Chances

by

Regina Bishop

Copyright © 2021 by Regina Bishop
All rights reserved.
ISBN: 979-8-218-18788-0

No part of the publication may be reproduced, stored in a retrieval system, or transmitted in any form or by any means-electronic, mechanical, photocopy, recording-or any other-except for brief quotations in printed reviews without the prior written permission of Regina Bishop.

This is a work of fiction. Names, characters, businesses, events, and incidents are the products of the author's imagination. Any resemblance to actual persons, living or dead, or actual events is purely coincidental.

Do everything in love, and I'll walk through fire for you.

ACKNOWLEDGMENTS

Thank you to my family and friends for all your love and support.

Aunt Debra Jenkins author of 'In the Midst' for encouragement and coaching. Thank you for allowing me to use a few characters from your novel.

Emily Wilson, Wesley Bishop and DJ Sanders for technical support.

Chris Wilson for the beautiful front cover and Nina Collett for the back cover.

Most of all to Jesus Christ for saving my soul and dying on the cross for me.

DEDICATION

In Loving Memory

of

Sprocket

You inspired me to write this novel when you were taken and never returned. I am sorry you didn't get to live out your last days with us. I know you died of a broken heart, I could see it in your eyes. I walked through fire for you and fought hard, but justice was not served. You were so loving, smart and funny.
You filled our hearts with joy and were a great protector. The memories of you will live forever because the love in our hearts will never die. Sunalei until we meet on that Rainbow Bridge.

CONTENTS

1	Spirit Dancer	1
2	Perseverance	10
3	I Am Not Ashamed	17
4	Coming Home	27
5	New Beginnings	36
6	Timing is Everything	47
7	Decisions	54
8	Building Bridges	62
9	Taking Chances	71
10	Feeling Free	80
11	Love Endures	87
12	Submission	94
13	Time Marches On	100
14	Stand By Me	107
15	Hot Summer Nights	115
16	Key To My Heart	124
17	Cat Scratch Fever	131
18	Wild Horses	138
19	Fire Inside Me	144
20	Fighting Fire with Fire	152

21	Guardian Angel	157
22	Returning Home	168
23	Mending Fences	175
24	Watching Over Me	181
25	Leather and Lace	187
26	EPILOGUE	192

Regina Bishop

SPIRIT DANCER

"Girls come down from that tree. We need to cut Abi's birthday cake and get ready for tonight," Abi's mom, Gayle, yelled from the porch. She made her way down the steps of the cabin carrying a cake.

"Okay, we're coming." Abi yelled.

Abi's friends looked at her and said, "You still have to tell us about that kiss." The three girls flipped over a tree branch and landed on their feet.

"His name is Luke, but do not tell anybody. Promise me."

"Okay, we promise." The girls made their way to the picnic table and giggled as they went.

They were joined by Gayle, Abi's dad Tom, Uncle Burt, and Johnny a ranch hand.

Johnny said, "I can't believe you're fifteen today," as he reached for a drink.

"Yeah, me either. I'll be driving soon, and I can't wait to get me a muscle car." Abi sat down, assured she would someday have it.

Burt turned to Gayle and indicated, "You are gonna have your hands full, sis."

Gayle smiled and pulled back Abi's long black hair. "She's a good girl, and I'm not worried. She does keep us busy with all her training, but she's so worth it," as she kissed Abi's head. "What is this?"

Gayle held up a feather from Abi's hair.

"I found it in the loft. It's pretty, isn't it?"

"This is an owl's feather," she started taking it out of her hair. "We do not wear owl feathers. You know that Abi." She watched it float to the ground.

Abi looked up at her mom, "Sorry Mama." She looked at her friends Kate and Jayda. "I can't wait for tonight. I hope there are some cute guys at the rodeo."

Johnny replied, "Luke is still here, you can hang out with him."

The girls started to giggle again.

Abi put her finger to her lips for the girls to be hush-hush.

Tom rolled his eyes. "Oh my goodness, this day has come way too soon," he huffed. "You can't date until you're thirty."

"Dad," she groaned.

"Okay, I'll think about it when you turn thirty," he winked at her.

Burt sat down, looked at Abi, and assured her, "There will be plenty of guys at the rodeo, especially with the casino in town. There's new people everywhere now."

"Tom, I've been thinking we need to add more cabins, what do you think?"

"That's a good idea," he nodded. "We may as well benefit from some of the casino traffic."

Burt nodded. "I've been thinking we need more horses for the trail riding, too."

Gayle pushed the cake to Abi. "Candles are lit, my little sparrow. Make your wish."

It only took a few seconds for Abi to grin from ear to ear and blow out fifteen candles in one big blow.

Gayle took her picture.

Everyone clapped and sang Happy Birthday, while Burt strummed the tune on his guitar.

Gayle put her hands on her hips. "Can we talk business later? There is too much going on today," she said as she cut the cake and began to pass it out. "I have enough to worry about for one day. I'm worn out from the Powwow last night. It's just too much for one weekend."

Tom comforted her. "Okay mama, next year we can have the

rodeo a different weekend."

Abi teased Burt, "Maybe you'll find a cowgirl tonight. She won't be in the clan."

The girls giggled while eating their cake.

"I think it's time for me to go to work young lady," he reached and pulled her nose. "I don't have the time for a woman, being sheriff and working the ranch," he stood up and made a gesture toward the entrance.

Tom turned around. "Here comes the truck now."

A large truck and trailer made its way down the driveway toward them, and the trailer was loaded with bulls. Burt went to direct the driver where to unload the bulls and the girls finished their cake.

"Let's go watch them unload the bulls," Abi suggested.

"Abi, why don't you show the girls the stomp dance. Your dad recorded the music on my phone." She picked up her phone. "I'm glad you remember about the clan rules. You know Luke would be like a brother."

"I know mom."

"Abi show us the dance, we want see." Kate pleaded.

"Please." Jayda chimed in.

"Alright." Abi got up from the table, relieved for a distraction. She began to dance around the table.

"That's so cool." Jayda said.

"It's a lot better when I'm all dressed up. Now let's go see the bulls."

She did not want more conversation about Luke, afraid her mom might see right through her.

The girls got up from the table and ran toward the barn and loading ramps.

Several bulls ran down the shoot to a holding pen. Abi peered in at a bull. Suddenly the bull rushed toward the fence. Abi stood frozen. The other girls jumped backwards hastily. The bull stopped before ramming the fence and looked at Abi, pawed the ground, and snorted.

Johnny watched Abi and her friends, then he slowly walked toward them with his leisurely stride.

Jayda placed her hands on her hips. "Abi's not even scared of those big bulls."

"They scare me to death," Kate replied as she chewed at her

fingernail.

Johnny leaned over toward the girls. "Her grandmother called her Spirit Dancer. She believed Abi had a gift with the animals. I believe that Abi has faith God will keep her safe."

The girls moved closer to Abi.

Abi looked at them. "Don't be afraid. Do you guys want to help get the horses ready? They need to be groomed before the show."

"Yeah, we would love to help." They both nodded their heads yes.

The girls went in the stable and each one took a beautiful Andalusian horse out of a stall. The manes flowed as they walked or when the horses moved their heads.

Tom joined the girls with his quarter horse, Rocky.

The stables were bustling with ranch hands and participants for the rodeo.

The girls took their time combing through the horses' manes.

Abi looked at her watch, "Where has the time gone? I have to go get ready." She laid her brush down. "I'll see y'all in a jiffy." She turned to run to a cabin, but Luke was standing directly in front of her. She stopped and looked at him, and they smiled at each other.

"I can help while you are getting ready," suggested the handsome young man.

"Sure, no problem," Abi pointed to the brush. "I appreciate your help."

When Abi returned, she had braided her long black hair, and her outfit was shiny red with sequins on the top. Gayle came down and was dressed like Abi. Each horse had a trick saddle donned on its back.

Gayle approached Abi. "Don't go far. After the parade we are the opening act."

"Okay, mom. I just want to go see where Jayda and Kate are sitting." She ran backward. "I'll be right back."

Gayle checked all the saddles.

Abi returned and Tom helped her onto the horse. "You be careful out there, I love you," he said.

"I will, Dad. I love you, too."

The event announcer asked everyone to stand for prayer and the National Anthem. Abi, Gayle, and Tom joined hands and prayed for everyone's safety. They each rode an Andalusian horse for the parade. After the arena cleared, Gayle and Abi went to the entry of the arena.

"Let's give a big welcome for Gayle Turner and her Andalusian horses," the announcer shouted.

Gayle went into the arena standing on the middle horse and she made a trip around the arena. She started moving the horses around each other. Sometimes she switched from one horse to another. They moved in sync and jumped over fire. She ended her act with one horse after she added a long, red, feather skirt to her attire. The horse went to the center of the arena and danced. When the song ended, Gayle stayed in the center and bowed to the crowd.

"That's my cue!" Abi sprinted into the arena standing on her saddle.

"Let's welcome Abigail Turner, daughter of Gayle and Tom Turner. She's been training since she was two, and today is her fifteenth birthday!"

The crowd stood and cheered as she waved.

She went into a 'one foot stand fly away', with the announcer shouting out each trick as she trotted around the arena.

"This one is a 'layout fender,' also known as an 'Indian Hideaway.'"

She made her way around in a 'forward fender,' then reversed to a 'backward fender.' Gayle turned as she passed to keep a watchful eye on Abi.

"The next one is a 'suicide drag.'" Abi hung backward off the side with one leg hanging outward. "She's picking up her hickory bow, that means she's doing a 'shroud layout' while shooting her bow. This is very difficult, folks. Let's see if she hits her target," said the announcer.

Abi was literally standing on the side of the horse and pulled back the arrow. The horse slowly galloped around the arena. The crowd was silent. She held her breath and let go of the arrow at the precise moment.

The announcer blared out, "She hit her target!"

The crowd came to their feet and cheered.

"This takes tremendous athleticism, folks."

Gayle and Abi circled the arena one more time together.

"Give another round of applause to Gayle and Abigail Turner!"

Jayda and Kate came running and squealing to meet Abi. "That was awesome!"

"I can't believe you hit the target!"

"Me either!" Abi shrieked as she jumped up and down.

Abi, Gayle and Tom embraced each other.

Burt gave a high five to everybody. "Good job." He turned to Tom. "You go out before bull riding, be safe out there."

He nodded, "I will."

Abi looked at Jayda and Kate. "I'm going to change into my jeans. I'll meet you at your seats!"

She darted toward a cabin.

Gayle and Tom kissed and held each other tight.

"I love you. You and Abi are the love of my life. She reminds me a lot of you out there."

"I love you, too. I thank God for both of you."

Moments later Abi ran into the stable and planted a big kiss on her dad's cheek. "I love you, Dad. I'm watching from right in the middle of the third row."

Gayle sprinted to the cabin to change. Soon after she joined the girls to watch the events. She also noticed Burt talking to two guys in suits but was quickly distracted by the bucking broncos. She was also keeping an eye on Abi sitting by Luke.

Soon the lights went out, a bull was released. The spotlight was on the bull.

"Ladies and gentlemen, here at Paradise Ranch we have the privilege of our very own matador, Mr. Tom Turner!"

The spotlight went to Tom. The audience cheered.

Gayle smiled at Abi and clapped. "Look, he's so handsome."

Tom moved closer to the bull and began to wave the muleta. The bull charged again and again.

Gayle watched nervously. "He makes it look so easy. It's like he's dancing with the devil."

"He'll be okay, Mom."

He maneuvered all around the bull.

"It feels like he's out there for an eternity."

He narrowly missed being gored. Gayle gasped and put her hands over her mouth to keep from screaming. Tom continued to taunt the bull and pouted out his lip, waiving the muleta.

The bull charged, kicked and twisted in the air, narrowly missing Tom again. The bull turned right and then left with his head. This time a horn caught Tom in the leg and knocked him to the ground.

The bull lowered his head and pawed at the ground as the dirt began to fly.

Abi ran to the fence and screamed. "Nooooo!" It eerily echoed through the valley.

The bull was distracted, and Tom got to his feet, to the safety of the fence. The bull was driven from the arena by the cowhands. Tom climbed down from the fence and bowed to the crowd. They stood and applauded.

He turned and limped toward the stable.

~~~~~

Gayle and Abi ran to meet him, desperate to get to him. "Are you okay?"

He waved at her, "I'm okay." He looked at his torn pants.

Gayle hugged him. "That's going to be sore."

"Yep," he grimaced.

"Dad are you sure you are okay," asked Abi.

"I'm fine sweetheart," he and Abi fist bumped.

"I told you he would be okay. Mom, I'm going back to watch the bull riders."

"Okay, we'll load the horses. We need to leave as soon as it's over. You have church tomorrow if you girls want to ride after that."

"Okay." Abi left the stable.

Tom reached for a horse. "I'm only taking the Andalusian's. I'll get Rocky tomorrow." He started to lead the horse to the trailer.

Gayle went to the cabin to gather some belongings. When she and Abi returned, Burt and Tom were talking.

"We'll talk about it later." Burt turned to Abi. "I'm so proud of you."

Abi gave Burt a hug. "I'll see you tomorrow," she said as she climbed in the truck.

Gayle kissed Burt on the cheek. "I'm so blessed and thankful it was a good night for everybody."

"Me too, sunalei (see you later)," Burt shut the truck door.

Abi laid in the back seat and yawned, "I'm so tired."

"We'll be home soon." Tom said as the truck began to move.

~~~~~

About an hour later, Burt and Johnny stood talking and heard an owl's loud screech.

"I don't like the sound of that," Burt looked around for the owl.

"Me either, bad omen," Johnny looked around.

Burt's phone rang. Burt motioned to get in the sheriff's car. They ran to the car. Lights and sirens blasted through the foggy night air as the black Dodge charger raced down the highway.

"800, do you have a copy?"

"10-4."

"Go directly to the hospital."

"10-4."

~~~~~

Burt pulled into the ER and burst into the trauma area. A deputy grabbed him by the shoulders and stopped him. "Let them do their job Burt, you can't go in there." The deputy struggled to hold him back.

Burt paced in front of the room. A few minutes later the doctor came out and sighed.

"I'm so sorry Burt, we lost both of them."

"But there was three in that vehicle," replied Burt.

"We have two adults, a male and female," the doctor indicated.

"Then where's Abigail?" he held his head.

The EMT said, "No other person was on the scene. It's a mess out there, even the horses didn't survive."

"Abi's still out there!" Burt turned and ran to the Charger with Johnny right behind him.

"This is 800, in route to the scene of 10-50 on 441 South, possible victim left at scene. Dispatch the chopper."

~~~~~

Abigail was lying on her back, and she looked up at the stars. When she closed her eyes, she began to drift away. She could she the angel wings as she seemed to float across the blue unknown. She was not afraid, and there was no pain. All she could feel was love and peace. There was no sense of space and time. It was beautiful, and many colors swirled around her that sparkled. She could see a light and she drifted toward the light. She could see her parents and they smiled and waved to her.

A bright light surrounded her and with it a magnificent white horse appeared. She heard a voice say, "BE STILL AND KNOW THAT I AM GOD."

Abigail could hear the pounding of horse hooves against the earth, and the sound of waves as if she were on the beach.

~~~~~

Burt pulled into a gruesome scene and talked to the officers there. Johnny looked out in the field and caught sight of a white horse rearing up. It pawed at the ground and did so for a few minutes. The horse ran forward, reared up and neighed. It ran back to the same spot, pawing.

"I think I know where Abigail is!" Johnny ran toward the horse, and the others followed him. The horse turned and ran, quickly disappearing into the early morning fog.

Abigail's body lay perfectly still in the grass. Burt assessed her pulse. "She's alive."

The chopper was directed to land. Abigail was stabilized and loaded.

Burt directed them, "Take her to Northeast Georgia Medical Center." He looked at his deputy. "Make sure every inch of this scene is gone over with a fine-toothed comb."

"Yes, sir." The deputy walked with Burt to the charger.

"Leak nothing about the victims to the press." He opened the car door and got in. "All media goes through me." He sped away from the scene with lights and sirens blasting again.

PERSERVERANCE

3 Days Later

The headlines of the paper read 'Three Family Members Killed in Horrific Accident.' Burt could not even bring himself to read the article he was so stricken with grief and laid it down. He heard a vehicle coming down the driveway and looked out the door. It was his deputy and a black sedan.

Deputy Fletcher walked up the steps and shook Burt's hand. "How you doing, man?"

Burt sighed. "Holding on by a thin thread."

"These guys are from the SBI." He made the introductions.

"Our condolences, Sheriff." They shook hands. "It's routine that we were called in on this. We have to ask; do you have any idea of anyone that would want to harm your family?"

His hands rested on his hips. "No, but I'm sure it wouldn't hurt to look at recent prison releasees."

Deputy Fletcher stated, "This was no accident, Sheriff. We found a slug in one of the tires and the brakes were tampered with."

One of the agents held his hand out. "That's why there were no skid marks on the scene."

Burt rubbed his face. "You gotta be kidding me." He hesitated then said, "Walk this way."

They proceeded to where Tom parked the night of the rodeo. Burt squatted and felt of the grass. He rubbed his fingers together and smelled the greasy substance. "Brake fluid." He stood up and angrily kicked the fence. "I'll be damned. They did it during the rodeo!"

The agents handed Burt their business cards. "We'll be in touch." They turned and walked away.

Burt kicked the fence again, breaking the board. He held to the top board and shook it as he wailed out in anger. He choked back the tears as he said, "Fletcher, can you keep an eye on this place? I'm gonna be out of town after tomorrow."

"Absolutely."

"You know Johnny, he'll be here."

"Yes, sir. I'll keep you posted."

~~~~~

Immediately after the celebration of life service, Burt headed south. He walked down a long hallway and met a man slightly younger than himself. The two men spread their arms and hugged, shaking each other. Burt looked at the name by the door. Jane Doe. "How is she?"

The man rubbed his head. "Doc said she's stable, goin' to be sore when she wakes up."

They both walked through the door and peered inside. A lady sitting in a recliner bounded to her feet and Burt embraced her. "It's good to see you, Hope."

"You, too." she answered subtly.

Burt said, "I can't thank y'all enough for this."

James assured him, "I had your back in Afghanistan, bro. I got your back now."

Both men simultaneously said, "Hooah."

Their attention turned to Abigail, lying in bed, sleeping. IVs were hanging everywhere, and the nurse came in to hang more. "These are antibiotics." she informed them. The room was quiet as they watched her. "I have to look at her incision." She gently rolled Abi to her side.

Abi slightly moaned.

"Everything looks good, it's clean and dry." She rolled her back again.

Burt folded his arms over his chest. "When do you think she'll wake up?"

The nurse shrugged. "Could be any minute. We have decreased the pain meds that make her so sleepy."

Hope said, "Thank you."

The nurse smiled and departed the room.

Burt, James, and Hope settled in the room waiting anxiously for Abi to arouse. Burt put his hands together and leaned forward to rest his forearms on his knees. "I don't know how I'm going to be able to tell her", his voice crackled.

"God will give you the right words when it's time," Hope nodded to reassure Burt.

"Speaking of the right words, I need y'all to understand what's going on. This was no freak accident," he straightened his back and placed his hands on his knees. "There was foul play." He stood and began to pace, rubbing his head. "I have to protect her."

Hope and James looked at each other and nodded.

James stood and put his hand on Burt's shoulder. "Consider it done. We will protect her," he claimed adamantly.

Burt desperately pleaded. "There has to be absolute secrecy, including her name."

James indicated, "We understand."

The two men hugged.

Hope looked over at Abi and wiped away a tear.

"Money won't be an issue. Tom and Gayle had life insurance of significant amounts. I'll handle some of the legalities and paperwork."

~~~~~

Burt went back to being sheriff, confident Abi, now Sierra, was on the mend and in good hands.

"Sheriff, you have some visitors," Beth announced.

"Show them in, please." Burt stood from behind his desk.

"This is Alan Dabadee and Carlos Cilia."

The two men shook hands with Burt. "We heard about your family. First, we want to offer our condolences."

Burt nodded, "Thank you. What can I do for you today?"

"We operate the Highlander Hotel and Casino."

Burt folded his arms across his chest and sat down. "I thought I recognized you two."

"We're businessmen, and we know it's too soon after your loss, but since we own the property next to your sister's property," he paused.

The other man finished, "Please come to us first, if you decide to sell."

Burt came to his feet stunned. He stuttered. "It is...early...I haven't made any...decisions yet." He showed them to the door with a scowl on his face and annoyed. "I'll know right where to find you fellas."

Beth looked on as the men left.

"Beth, can you get Ari Fletcher in here?" He went back to his office and shut the door. He sat at his desk rubbing his head.

"Sheriff, you have a call from Sierra Wilson, do you want to take it?" Beth asked.

"Yes."

Before Beth hung up, she heard Burt. "Hey baby. How are you feeling?"

"A little sore, but I'm taking therapy and getting stronger."

"Good, you work hard and stick with it."

"I will, I miss you. Can you come out this weekend?"

There was a knock at the door.

"I probably can. I'll call you later, okay. Gotta go." Burt said, hanging up the receiver. "Come in...shut the door, have a seat."

"What's up?" Ari Fletcher asked as he sat down and crossed his legs.

"I had some visitors from that damn casino. I remembered at the rodeo I had two guys show up from there. They asked to meet about a business proposition."

Ari leaned to one side and rested his chin in his hand. "What do you want to do?"

~~~~~

The weekend arrived and Burt informed Johnny he was going out of town. Burt loaded his luggage and then Dixie, a blonde cocker spaniel that belonged to Abi. Johnny noticed he took the dog and smiled, but never said a word.

~~~~~

Burt headed east to a little town called Dallas. He pulled into a nice spread and was met by Sierra. Burt tried to get out the door, but Dixie climbed into his lap, tail wagging and her whole body shaking. The door opened and Sierra and Dixie were reunited.

Sierra rubbed Dixie's ears. "Hey girl! I missed you so much." Dixie jumped down from the vehicle and Sierra followed after her.

Hope had her hands in the middle of her back. "I haven't seen her this happy since she came here. She really needed this."

"How do you think she's adjusting?"

"Sometimes she just sits quietly and stares in space. She hasn't really opened up yet. I'm giving her time to come around on her own."

James chimed in, "We try to keep her busy. Hey Sierra, would you like to show Burt what we've been working on?"

"Sure," she hobbled in the house on crutches and Dixie followed her.

She came back out to the yard carrying a black case. She took out a 9mm pistol and loaded it.

"Do you see that target over there?" She pointed the gun.

"Yeah." Burt looked where she was pointing.

Sierra fired several rounds, hitting the bullseye every shot.

"Good job young lady. Wow, you're a natural." Burt clapped.

"Dad always said 'aim small, miss small.'"

"That reminds me, I brought your bow. It's still in the truck."

~~~~~

The next day was Sunday, and everyone was sitting around the table. "Sierra, do you want to go to church?" Hope asked and sipped her coffee.

"I don't think so since Burt's here." She got up from the table.

"Don't stay on my account, I'll go with you," he sipped his coffee and turned to look at her.

She looked out the window. "It's just that right now, I'm kinda mad at God and I don't understand why bad things happen to good people." She turned to look at all of them. "I miss my friends, why can't I call them?"

"No." replied Burt.

Sierra pleaded, "At least let me call Luke. You said he was like a brother."

"No. We can't risk you calling your friends, I'm sorry. Not even Luke, he's still a kid. He won't understand." Burt said, "And don't be mad at God. God is good. He saved you. You have a purpose on this earth. None of us is promised tomorrow."

Sierra stormed out of the house crying.

James asked, "Has Johnny figured it out yet?"

"Probably, you know I can't hide anything from him, but he hasn't said anything."

Hope placed her hand on Burt's arm. "I'll go talk to her." She stood up and followed Sierra outside.

~~~~~

Hope approached Sierra. "Would you like to talk?" She waited for an answer.

Sierra shrugged her shoulders and sniffled.

"We don't always understand what God's plan is. He works in mysterious ways. We have to trust him," she paused. "Sometimes Christians suffer so it draws us closer in our relationship with God."

Sierra stared out in the pasture. "It's not fair and I don't understand. I keep having a dream of a big white horse standing over me."

"I think in time you will understand." Hope offered her a hand. "Come in the house, I have something to show you." They went inside.

~~~~~

Hope handed Sierra a frame. "Your mother gave me this when we were about your age."

Sierra read out loud, "Footprints in the Sand."

"So, you see, you're not alone. That was one of your mom's favorites, and I've kept it all these years," as Hope sat on the bed.

"Why did Mama give it to you?"

"My little sister died of cancer, and I can remember feeling about the same way you feel now."

"I'm sorry, I didn't know." She looked up at her.

"It's okay. I know she isn't suffering anymore and that she's with Jesus. Someday I will see her again."

"Just like me. I'll see Mama and Daddy again."

"You sure will."

Sierra held the frame to her chest. "Can I keep it for a while?"

"Sure."

Sierra walked over to the dresser and sat the frame down. "Why don't I dream about my parents? I dream of everything else."

Hope stood up and walked over to Sierra. "Because I believe they are at peace, and they wouldn't want you to be worried about them." Hope put her arms around Sierra's shoulders.

She looked up at her. "What do you think it means about the big white horse?"

"I don't know, but as time goes by, I think you'll find your answer." She tapped her nose with her finger. "Just be patient and listen. Take one day at a time. You have to get better first. We start home school tomorrow."

"Good. I don't want to go to school on crutches. Everybody will stare at me," she looked down.

Hope stroked her hair. "You can go to school next year and no one will ever know. A few months of therapy and you will be good as new."

"But I have to keep my grade average an A so I can get into a good veterinarian school. Did you know that was what I have wanted to do my whole life?"

"Your mom mentioned it. I think it suits you. Meanwhile, this summer we are going to have a blast in the pool."

Sierra smiled at Hope. "That will be something I've never had, a pool."

"Well, it's something for you to look forward to."

I AM NOT ASHAMED

15 YEARS LATER

Beep, beep, beep, beep. Sierra reached for the snooze button and slipped back into a deep sleep. She was in an open field, walking slowly and unsure of where she was. Fog was all around her. She heard a snort and hooves pounded against the ground. She turned in all directions but couldn't see anything. From out of the fog, a large black bull with horns charged straight at her. Time stood still and in her moment of hesitation the bull's horn caught her in the back.

Suddenly she was wide awake, standing by her bed. She reached to her back and rubbed out a spasm. Beep, beep, beep, she turned the alarm off. She groaned and flopped back on the bed.

This time she was disturbed by an ambulance's siren blaring down the road in front of her apartment. She covered her head with a pillow. "Lord, please help me remember nothing is going to happen today that You and I can't handle. Amen."

She quickly scurried about her morning routine drinking her Mountain Dew. "Today has to be a ponytail day," she said as she pulled her long black hair from around her pretty face. She put on some mascara.

She pulled out a pair of scrubs from the closet and tossed them on the bed. Her eye caught a glimpse of a four-inch scar right in the center of her back, in the mirror hanging on the bathroom door. She paused before putting on her scrubs and tuned to look closer in the mirror. "Love yourself first or no one else will," she said out loud.

'I look more like my mom every day.' She thought as she flexed her muscles in front of the mirror. Every muscle in her body was well defined on her 5'9" frame. "Mom wasn't this muscular." She turned off the radio, pulled on her scrubs, and looked at the clock. "Great, I'm late."

~~~~~

Moments later she was sitting in her Chevy Camaro in heavy traffic. She turned on the radio for a traffic report. There was an accident at the next intersection.

"Goodness gracious." She turned to take and alternate route. Again, she was snarled in heavy traffic. "Can anybody drive worth a darn?"

Her phone rang and she picked it up. "This is Dr. Wilson; can I help you?"

"Hey, it's Bobbie at work. Just wondering when you might get here."

"I'm stuck in traffic on the 400, but I've moved some. Maybe fifteen more minutes?" She looked around at the traffic.

"We have a dog here someone dropped off and he's pretty bad. I don't know if he'll make it. He's been set on fire."

"Where's Dr. Vargas?" She squeezed her temples.

"He's not coming in till noon today."

"Great, wouldn't you know it? He could at least call me and give me a heads up." She darted into another lane, horns blowing.

~~~~~

The staff at the vet. clinic worked diligently to keep the dog alive until Sierra arrived. Upon entering the clinic, Sierra tossed her Nave' bag into the office and rushed to the room of the charred dog.

Her eyes fell on the poor creature. "Oh Jesus, Jesus, Jesus," she wrapped her hands around his face.

He opened his eyes and began to lick her hands. There was a slight wag of his stubby tail. The hair across his back was completely gone and large blisters covered the area. Sierra sedated the dog and began treatment.

"He's got a 50/50 chance, I think," she said as she washed her hands.

"Good," Bobbie said.

"Contact the police and let's see if they can find out anything." Bobbie wrapped him in a blanket. "What kind of dog is he?"

"Cattle dog. He's probably not from around here." She cleaned off the sink.

Bobbie picked him up. "He's pitiful, but he's got to be the ugliest dog I've ever seen."

"Well, he makes up for it in smarts," and Sierra walked out of the room.

~~~~~

Sierra entered a treatment room with a young woman sitting and waiting patiently. There was a crate on a table with a blanket over it.

"Hello," the woman said uneasily.

"Hello, what do we have here?"

"It's my daughter's cat. She's so aggressive we can't do anything with her. She attacks everybody in the house." She shook her head. "I don't know what to do."

Sierra pulled back the blanket. The black cat swatted and squalled. She pulled the blanket down again. "This is gonna be a tough one. We'll get her settled in and watch her. I can't examine her right now. I'll call you, okay?"

The woman sighed. "Okay."

"What's her name?"

"Pebbles."

"Bobbie, can you put Pebbles in the behavioral room and just open the crate door. Let her come out on her own. Put some food and water in there. Let's see if she'll eat."

"Okay," Bobbie reached for the crate.

Sierra continued with her morning seeing several clients, her back wrenched in pain.

Bobbie asked, "Are you alright?"

Sierra stretched. "I guess for getting butted out of the bed by a bull this morning."

Bobbie wrinkled her brow. "What?"

"Never mind," she rubbed her back.

The police officer walked in.

Sierra greeted him and told the story of the burned dog. They walked back to his location.

"Someone put diesel on him. He's not chipped. I can't imagine where he would belong around here. He's a cattle dog." She pulled back the blanket.

"Whoa, that's one ugly dog," he looked at the dog on the blanket.

She covered him up and raised her eyebrows, rolling her eyes.

"We'll do what we can, but with nothing to go on it's pretty much hopeless." He held out his hand and note pad.

"I know what that means." She turned to walk away. "Thanks anyway."

~~~~~

Sierra sat down to eat her lunch.

Dr. Vargas appeared in the doorway. His hair was tussled, his clothes wrinkled, and his shirt untucked. Sierra smelled alcohol across the room. "You look like crap," she informed him.

"I'm at work, ain't I? It's my clinic, I'll dress like crap if I want to. Just be glad you gotta' job." He staggered away.

Sierra felt the steam coming out of her ears. She wanted to scream at him, but had to grit her teeth, and maintain her composure. She tried to finish her sandwich, but it seemed to grow in her mouth. She spit it in the garbage can by her desk.

"Jesus H. Christ! Sierra, get in here!"

She was startled but got up and headed to another room.

~~~~~

"This dog is three fourths' dead. Why did you treat him when there is no owner?!" He paced the floor. "We don't run a free clinic here."

"I'll pay for the dog's treatment then. I felt like he had a 50/50 chance. He responded well to me when I got here," she veered at him.

He held his hands out. "You can't save them all! I know you think you can, but you can't," he was inches from her face.

She turned her head to the side to avoid the alcohol breath. "I had to try, he deserved a chance." She cut her eyes toward Dr. Vargas.

"If you want to be in partnership next year, you need to learn to let some go." He walked away.

The staff looked at Sierra.

The rest of the day was never-ending. Once Dr. Vargas got to work the air was so thick you could cut it with a knife. Hardly anybody spoke to each other, and nobody laughed. Sierra couldn't wait to get home that day.

~~~~~

Sierra left work, turned the radio up loud to Lynyrd Skynyrd, 'Three Steps.' She went home and changed clothes and got out her 9mm pistol and compound bow.

~~~~~

Sierra went to the shooting range. In her mind, she was hitting Dr. Vargas right between the eyes every shot she took. She thought, 'What happened to him? He is a changed person from when I started working with him. I really don't want to be partners.' She muttered as she fired, "Jekyll and Hyde." She fired again, "from one minute to the next."

Some guys watched her, but she didn't even notice.

"She's mad at somebody."

"Glad it's not me, she's a bad ass."

~~~~~

That night before going to bed, she prayed for guidance. She thought of her parents and the North Carolina mountains as she drifted off to sleep.

~~~~~

The rest of the week was like walking on eggshells. The best part of the week was seeing the burned dog dramatically improved. She looked in on him. "Hey buddy."

He wagged his tail.

Bobbie walked by. "I can't believe how that dog reacts to you every time. You truly have a gift with the animals."

"Let's see how Pebbles is doing." They entered the room. Sierra sat down in the middle of the room. Pebbles rubbed up against her, purring.

Sierra examined her without being clawed or any problems.

"See what I mean?" Bobbie said.

Sierra got up from the floor. "Call Pebbles owner. Let's see what's going on at home. I'm willing to bet she's in a hostile environment."

Bobbie called. "The phone is disconnected."

"Well, isn't that par for the course?" They left the room. "That reminds me, I need to go get a new phone before we go to Cross-Fit. Do you mind? It won't take long."

"No, that's fine."

~~~~~

On the way to the phone company Bobbie said, "What are you going to do with that cattle dog? I thought you couldn't have pets."

"I can't and now it looks like I'm going to have a cat too, if Pebble's owner doesn't show up. If I could have a dog, I wanted a beagle. They're really smart and cute."

"You just need to buy a place. Don't you board your horses anyway?"

"I sure do, but truth be told, I don't think I belong in the city. I hear the mountains calling my name." She looked at her. "I could open my own clinic and not have to put up with ole' sour puss every day." They both laughed.

"That sounds great. You should go for it. I heard his kids do drugs and him and his wife are getting a divorce," Bobbie said.

"How come nobody has told me?" Sierra looked at her.

"Figured you knew, I guess." She pulled in a parking spot.

Sierra hesitated to get out of the car. "Well, that explains a lot. It all makes sense now."

~~~~~

The store was jammed full of people. Bobbie looked around. "What are they doing?...Giving away free phones?"

Sierra looked around, "This line is never-ending."

"There's too many Mexicans in here," Bobbie whispered.

Sierra was taken aback by Bobbie's comment. She thought, 'how can I address it without hurting her feelings?' "I can always come back tomorrow," she looked at Bobbie.

She shrugged her shoulders, "It's up to you."

Sierra motioned toward the door with her hand as she headed toward the door.

~~~~~

They walked to the car. "You know, my dad was Spanish-American. That's how come I know Spanish."

"I'm sorry, I didn't mean anything by it. I thought you were Native American."

"My mom was Cherokee."

"How did your mom and dad meet?"

They got in the car. "They both performed in the rodeo circuit. My mom and dad always said they fell in love the first moment they met. They wouldn't see each other for weeks or months at a time, they couldn't stop thinking about each other. They said they could feel each other no matter how far apart they were."

"I guess absence really does make the heart grow fonder."

"I suppose it does. I just hope that someday I can find the kind of love like they shared. Changing the subject back to the race thing. The biggest thing that bothers me with the race issue is when people think the Indians don't belong here. My people were driven from North Carolina. You know the trail of tears story. The Eastern Band of Cherokee is getting so small it's barely a tribe anymore. I like being multi-racial," she boasted. "I feel like I can fit anywhere. I also feel like I don't belong anywhere."

There was silence sitting at the red light.

Sierra looked at Bobbie, "I'm willing to bet that you can't tell if Jesus is red, yellow, black, or white." They both laughed. "Seriously what if I told you we were all just beings of light and your soul is what matters."

"I've never thought about it like that, but it is an interesting perspective."

"You're really smart. When were you born?"

"March 20th."

"You were born at the end of the life cycle, that's why you're so smart."

"Is that a good thing?" Sierra inquired.

"Not necessarily, it takes a lifetime to acquire knowledge. Pisces are very patient people. Your birthday falls right between the end of the life cycle and the beginning, it's called the cusp between two signs. That's the fire inside of you. When you've had all you can take, then you take more, and then you explode," she did an explosion motion with her hands. "You are also a dreamer and a doer."

"How do you know all this?"

She pulled in a parking spot. "Just a hobby. I like to study different ideas about life. I do wonder sometimes if I'm on the right life path. How about you, do you ever wonder if you're doing what you were put here to do?"

"Maybe," she paused. "I want my life to matter, I do know that. I wonder why there are so many missing and murdered indigenous women and no one seems to think they matter. They don't get the publicity like when it's someone else and that really bothers me."

"Really, I had no idea it was that way."

"Case and point but I have my own theory. You sure pegged me on the personality thing. Most people just remember the explosion parts," she laughed. "I really don't celebrate my birthday too much, I've always been in college or working." She gathered up her bag.

They got out of the car.

"My birthday was the day of my accident and it's a grim reminder of my parents being killed," they walked toward the gym.

"I'm so sorry, I had no idea."

"It's okay, I don't talk about this kind of stuff too much."

~~~~~

Sierra came out in a sporty ensemble.

Bobbie stared at her. "I didn't know you were so buff. You can't tell underneath those pajamas we wear every day."

"I've spent my whole life to get here. I have to work out to keep my pain level down." She pointed which way to go. "It's getting harder to deal with. I'm having some shots in my back Thursday, so I'll be out of work for two days," she turned around.

Bobbie could see the scar. She wanted to ask what happened but was hesitant. Sierra didn't offer to tell her.

"Oh, don't let me forget to tell Vargas tomorrow, he'll have a duck fit." She smiled and picked up the ropes. She slammed them against the floor.

"What kind of shots, cortisone?"

"No, it's called platelet rich plasma (PRP) for short. They draw your blood and spin it real fast. They take the plasma and inject it in the painful area to make new tissue grow."

"You look like a picture of health. It's hard to believe you're in pain." She swung a Kettle Bell between her legs and up and back.

"Looks are deceiving sometimes. You know what they say, never judge a book by the cover."

"I guess you never know what someone else is going through," Bobbie suggested.

Sierra punched a bag several times, then kicked it. "That's what I always say. That's why you should always treat people with kindness, you know…how you would want to be treated."

"Nobody lives by that golden rule anymore, it's all about me, me, me, and more me."

Sierra kicked the bag. "You got that right. Tomorrow's cardio day if you want to go run in the park with me. You're welcome to come."

"Where do you find time for all this? I don't see how you do it."

"I've always been active and training in something. You just have to want it and you make it happen…manage your time," she flipped a tire.

Bobbie watched her.

"I got a little slack going through vet school…my pain got so bad…it was hard to get under control…I got real depressed, too…don't want to go there again…Psych meds will kill you…and narcotics." She wiped her brow.

Bobbie noticed all the people watching Sierra, but she was completely oblivious to any attention she was drawing.

"Ooowhee, that really gets my right leg going." She stopped to drink some water. "It's my weak leg."

Bobbie muttered, "I'm exhausted."

"Let's call it a day, then. We did good." They gave each other a high five.

~~~~~

The next day at the end of the day, most employees had already left for the day.

"Sierra, can you see me before you leave?" Vargas said as he walked by her door.

She thought, 'What now? It's like being called to the principal's office and you know you haven't done anything wrong.'

A few minutes later she went to his office. "Sir, you wanted to see me?"

"I've been going over our numbers since it's getting close to the end of the year. I really don't see a way of keeping you here next year, let alone making you a partner," he showed no emotion at all.

"But I've kept this clinic going and I've worked my tail off for you, for four years. How can you do this to me and it's Christmas time?" she shrugged her shoulders and held out her hands.

"You're a good vet, you won't have any trouble finding another job." He turned his back to her.

"This is a blindside. How long has this been on your mind?"

There was a long pause, and he took a deep breath before he turned to look at her. "It's for the best."

"I don't know what's going on in your life, but you're a different person than you were four years ago. You swear all the time. You come in drunk. You just don't care anymore about anything." She waited for a reply.

He just raised his eyebrows and closed his eyes.

"This is not just a job to me. For me, it was a calling from God."

He was sarcastic, "Oh, please."

"You say I have a way with animals, you've seen it yourself. Well that's a God given talent and I am not ashamed." She paused before she turned to walk out. "I'm taking the diesel dog and black cat Pebbles."

~~~~~

That evening, Sierra took Diesel for a run in the park to blow off some steam. They were standing still to catch their breath. A passer-by said, "That's one ugly dog."

Diesel and Sierra looked at each other and they both cocked their head to the side with a half smirk on their faces. "Don't worry, buddy. I'm taking you to a place where you will be loved and very much appreciated." She rubbed his ears. He wagged his stubby tail.

~~~~~

That night, Sierra stared into space as she listened to calming music from a fan flute. She lit some candles and sat cross legged. She smudged herself with sage and began to meditate. Her mind drifted to her childhood in the mountains. She imagined sitting by the river and dipping her feet in the crystal cool waters and playing in the waterfalls. She remembered running through the open fields with the horses around her and laying in the field staring up at the stars. She could see her ancestors from long ago.

Her grandmother appeared to her and spoke in the native language, "Spirit Dancer you must wake up my child. It is time to raise your spirit. God has blessed you with many gifts."

When she opened her eyes, she couldn't explain the feeling she had, but knew that is was a sign for her to return home. She called Burt. "I lost my job today. I had already decided it was time I come home. I'm not a child anymore and I need some answers. I'm not hiding any longer."

"I wondered when you would be ready. I knew it was getting close so come home," Burt said. "You belong here."

COMING HOME

Back at the ranch, Johnny was feeding some cattle. Burt was checking on one particular heifer that was pregnant. Johnny stopped feeding and stood still. He looked south. A big grin came over his face. "A storm is coming."

Burt looked up in the Carolina blue sky. "You're crazy, old man," he said, as he went on about his business and grinned.

Johnny turned to look at him. "Waiting for a calf to be born is like watching paint dry. Now that's crazy."

~~~~~

Two days later, a jacked up white Chevy Silverado pulled into the ranch. Behind it was a horse trailer with three horses inside.

Sierra stood there, looked around and smelled the fresh country air. She let Diesel out and then Pebbles, "Siyooooo!" (Helloooooo!)

No one answered, so she headed to the stables. Inside she walked to a stall with a lone horse.

She ran her hand up his nose to his mane, "Rocky?"

"No, that's Duke. Rocky was his dad," Johnny peeked over the loft.

"Oh, you scared me," she looked up at him. "I didn't think anyone was here."

Johnny climbed down from the loft.

Sierra stepped over to greet him with a handshake. "Hi, I'm Sierra."

He looked at her funny. "I know who you are, Abigail Turner."

"Johnny!" She jumped into his arms. "I missed you!" She

grinned from ear to ear.

He swung her around. "I knew it all along, I could feel it in my bones."

"What are you feeling in your bones, old man?" Burt asked as he came around the corner, with a sheepish grin on his face.

Johnny reached down and picked up a horse biscuit and threw it at Burt. "You didn't hide nothing from me, you old buzzard."

All three laughed out loud.

"I knew when that white stallion was standing over you in that field that you were going to be alright." He folded his arms over his chest.

She laid her hand on his arm. "I still dream of that white stallion a lot. When I was laying there, I heard a voice telling me 'Be still and know that I am God,' and then you found me."

"I believe you. I went back down there a few times and I've never found a white horse anywhere ever."

Sierra smiled and put her other hand on his arm pulling him to the trailer, "Let's unload my horses."

They walked to her trailer.

"Are you here to visit, or stay?"

She opened the trailer door. "Oh, I'm staying."

Johnny looked at Burt and boasted, "I told you a storm was coming."

Burt raised his hand to tip his hat.

Sierra guided out each horse. "This is Raindancer, a paint. Duchess and Prince are Andalusian's." Diesel came bounding toward them. "And this is Diesel," she bent over and petted him. "Pebbles is a black cat running around here somewhere."

A sporty silver Camaro came down the driveway, followed by a moving truck. Hope and James got out. "We made it!"

"Hope you didn't have any trouble." Johnny said.

"No, we did okay." James replied.

Burt said to Sierra, "That one," he pointed to a cabin above his, "I built for you."

"Really?" She looked at the cabin and hugged him.

"It's more modern than the others. Go see if you like it." Burt motioned toward the cabin.

"I love it, I don't even have to look. You know what I like," she bounded up the hill to a rustic cabin with a porch.

They all stood and watched her.

She yelled and held her arms up. "It's perfect!" She admired the view of the mountains from the porch and breathed in fresh air.

Hope expressed her approval. "It really turned out nice."

James agreed. "It's good to see the finished product. I think she likes it."

"Go ahead, take a look inside," Burt motioned toward the cabin again.

Hope and James walked up the stone pathway.

Sierra gleamed with joy, "I love that stacked stone on the fireplace and the cherry mantle. It will match my furniture."

Hope rubbed her hands together. "It sure looks cozy and warm."

Burt came in carrying a Frazier fur and set it in the corner next to the fireplace. "Merry Christmas and welcome home."

She hugged him and kissed his cheek. "This place is awesome. Sgi (Thank you)."

~~~~~

The ranch was very busy the next few days. Hope and James stayed in a cabin of their own and helped Sierra get settled, including decorating for Christmas.

Hope peeked out the window. "I wonder who that is?"

A pickup truck pulled in at the barn. A man got out and walked to the barn.

Sierra looked just in time to see him enter the shadow of the barn. "Oh, that's the veterinarian, look at the side of the truck. He's probably checking on the pregnant heifer." She went back to decorating her mantle.

"You can go down there if you need a break."

Sierra looked over her shoulder at Hope. "I've been so busy I haven't been to the barn for two days. Thank God for Johnny and Burt."

"We're just about done, go on down there," Hope insisted.

"I think I'm going to run to town and pick up some pizzas for dinner." She put her hands on her hips. "I don't want to cook and get this pretty kitchen dirty." She held her hand out toward the room.

The kitchen had dark cherry cabinets with black appliances and granite counter tops. The handles on the cabinets were black. The walls were olive green, and there was a pretty back splash. The living room was painted a tan brushed suede look and trimmed out in white. The hardwood floors were dark cherry. The ceiling in the living room was vaulted.

~~~~~

Dr. Davenport was met in the barn by Diesel, and he reached down to pet him. "Hey buddy, where did you come from? You look like you've been scalded, but you're healing good." He walked toward Burt.

"That's Diesel, and yeah, he was burned after some idiot poured diesel on him. That's how he got his name."

Dr. Davenport looked back at him, "Well, he's got a good home now."

They walked toward the stall. "Let's take a look at that heifer."

The doctor examined the cow. "Well, any day now. She seems to be fine. Just leave her be and quit watching. Waiting for a calf to be born is like watching paint dry."

Burt raised his eyebrows and lifted the brim of his hat.

~~~~~

Sierra went to town and pulled in at the Indian Mound Restaurant. A Hummer was parked across three spaces right in front of the door. Sierra parked at the rear of the vehicle, and a work truck pulled in at the front of the Hummer. Sierra pulled her parka hood over her head and walked to the door.

A woman came out the door in a hurry. She pushed the door into Sierra and didn't acknowledge her. She carried several pizzas and was on her cell phone. She had a strong northern accent. "I don't believe this. These hillbillies have blocked me in. I'll have to call you back."

Sierra stood and watched. Three guys got out of the work truck.

"You need to move. Can't you see I'm parked here, you idiot."

One of the guys looked at her, the other two went toward the restaurant. The one moved the truck.

One of them said, "I can't stand her."

Sierra asked, "Who is she?"

"Some big wig from the casino." They watched her drive away, still on her phone.

"Not much in the Christmas spirit, is she?" another one said.

"She's probably atheist," Sierra replied.

They all laughed and went inside.

Sierra scrunched her furry hooded parka closer to her face. She took her pizzas, "See ya'll later."

"I hope so, let me get the door for you," as he reached for the door.

The three guys looked on as she climbed into her truck. She tried to hide her face and not make eye contact.

"The question is, who…are…you?" One guy said, "I like that truck."

One replied, "Lord, have mercy."

"Do you know her?" one turned to the cashier.

"No, she's probably visiting somebody for the holidays, but she looked Cherokee."

"Well, I sure hope to see Ms. Cherokee again."

The cashier rolled her eyes.

~~~~~

Sierra pulled on the highway and noticed her old dance studio still there. 'I wonder where Jayda, Kate, Pam, and Amya are? Would they even remember me? What would it be like to see them again?'

Her eyes filled with tears as she drove away.

~~~~~

Sierra returned with the pizza and went to the barn. "Guys, I've got pizza. Come and eat," she walked further in. "How's the mamma?"

"Dallas said it wouldn't be long and she looked good."

"Who is Dallas?" she inquired and placed her hands on her hips.

"The vet." Burt pushed his hat up as he looked up at her.

"Oh," she shrugged it off.

They all looked at her kind of funny. She turned around to leave, but Pebbles rubbed against her leg, and she picked her up. "You're okay."

Diesel watched over the mom to be with a vigilant eye and waited. Sierra gave each horse a pat on the neck as they munched on some grain. Everyone left the barn and closed the doors.

~~~~~

The next day Hope did some grocery shopping. Most of the day was spent cooking side dishes and desserts alongside Sierra. The cabin was cozy and warm with a soft glow from the fire. The Christmas tree sparkled. The aroma of fir tree mixed pleasantly with all kinds of home cooked goodies.

Sierra heard the wind whistle through the trees around back. She looked out the window to see big snowflakes dancing in the wind. "It's snowing," she chirped.

Hope said, "It would be nice to have a white Christmas," as she continued to cook, "but it's only going to flurry."

"I like seeing it snow on Christmas Eve." She kept looking out the window.

Christmas morning arrived and Sierra could smell the turkey breast she had put in the crock pot before going to bed.

She prayed, "Happy Birthday, Jesus, and thank you for all your blessings on this special day. Amen." She looked out the window first thing to see if it snowed, but it was only a dusting. "I wonder if the calf was born?" She splashed some cold water on her face and dressed in a hurry.

~~~~~

At the barn, she was disappointed there was no calf. She was greeted by the neighing of the horses, and she passed out some grain. "Osda sunalei" (Good morning).

~~~~~

The day was filled with laughter, exchange of gifts, good food, and love of her family. She thought, 'It was almost perfect.' Her eyes filled with tears when she thought of her parents and as she stared into the fire.

Hope noticed Sierra wipe away some tears. "It's okay to cry, you don't have to be strong all the time." She stood by her.

"I think I just got some mascara in my eye. I'm really tired, I'm about ready to go to bed."

Burt got up from the recliner. "We're all tired, I think that's a good idea," he stretched. "It has been a busy and hectic few days. I know I'm ready to turn in myself."

Everyone said goodnight and they all went to their cabins.

~~~~~

About 4:00 am, Diesel pawed at Sierra's door and barked. Sierra threw on her fluffy white robe and went to the door. Diesel was running to the barn and back to Sierra.

Sierra slipped on some furry boots sitting by the door. She ran down the pathway. "Go get Burt, boy!" She pointed to his cabin.

Burt was coming out the door and got on his phone. They both knew something was wrong.

~~~~~

They entered the barn to find the mama cow was barely breathing.

Sierra looked at Burt hovered over the mama. "I don't know what to do. I don't know much about cows." She was frustrated and overwhelmed.

"Dallas is on his way; we've got to get that baby out or we'll lose both of 'em."

She put her hands on her head. "No, no, no!" Pebbles scurried to hide.

Burt went into action. "Hold her tail." He reached in and pulled out a foot. "Oh, Jesus, help me." It slipped from his grip.

They both struggled to get a hold of the calf enough to make any progress. Sierra sat on the ground, braced her feet, and pulled with both hands. Burt maneuvered the head. One big pull and she pushed with her legs. The baby slipped out and landed in her lap.

At that moment Dallas walked in just in time to see the baby slide out. He could not believe his eyes. Sierra was covered in grunge, her white robe no longer recognizable. She rubbed the calf, trying to get it to move.

"It's a bull," Burt said, looking on.

"Come on, little guy, you can make it." Dallas started rubbing harder.

Sierra picked up his head and rubbed his face. "Please don't die. I know how you feel, I've been there." Her eyes teared up and her voice was shaky.

The little calf began to move and then a little more. They watched. Out came a tiny bleating sound. They all started to laugh, and Sierra cried at the same time.

"Thank you, Lord, thank you," she rubbed his head and the calf got up.

Dallas assisted Sierra to her feet. Sierra turned around and their eyes met, time stood still for a moment.

Burt rubbed the little black calf.

Dallas and Sierra stood there looking at each other, their hearts pounding.

"Good job," Dallas reached to move a strand of her hair.

"Thanks," she smiled and turned away from him.

"Sierra, Dallas, meet each other," Burt smiled. He pulled out a handkerchief and handed to her to wipe her face.

"Thanks," her eyes got big as she reached for the hanky.

Dallas was at least six feet tall and broad shouldered. His hair was wavy black, and his eyes were blue. He was clean shaven except for a thin line of a mustache and beard that outlined his jawline. He mixed a special formula in a big bottle and handed it to Sierra.

The calf began to suckle it. "He's strong," she said as she struggled to hold it.

Dallas stood behind her, his hands rested on the top of a stall gate.

Soon, the barn was hustling with Johnny, James, and Hope.

Sierra quietly slipped out and Diesel followed her. "Good job, boy. Good job," she petted him.

Sierra hurried to clean up, 'I bet I'll never see him again,' she thought.

Dallas anxiously lingered for her return and tried not to be obvious but couldn't hold it back.

"Who is Sierra?"

"Oh, she just moved in the cabin above mine." Burt said, and grinned at Hope, each tried to be nonchalant.

James petted Diesel, and tried to act like he didn't know anything either.

"I'll see y'all later today. I'll come back to check on the little guy," Dallas left before Sierra returned.

Sierra came to the barn all cleaned up. She walked straight to Burt and punched him in the shoulder.

"Ouch, what was that for?" he rubbed his shoulder.

Sierra put her hands on her hips. "You didn't tell me Dr. Davenport was so good looking. I figured he was some old man." She paced and threw her arms every which way. "He's only the hottest guy I've ever laid my eyes on."

They all watched her.

She held her hand out. "He probably thinks I crawled out from under a rock." She looked at each one of them. "You know, you only get one chance to make a good first impression, don't you?"

Everyone started to laugh at her.

She put her hands on her hips again. "It's not funny!"

James tried to ease her mind. "Trust me, you impressed him," he chuckled.

"He'll be back later today!" Burt yelled after her as she left the barn.

Hope said, "I tried, she insisted on going after pizza."

Later that day, Dallas did return. He looked at the calf. "He looks good, I brought more formula," he sat it down. "It's a good thing you have more time now, this little guy is going to keep you guys busy."

"Yep," Burt said and rubbed his head.

"How long were you sheriff?"

"Eighteen years," he stuffed his hands in his pockets, "a long time. I'm kinda glad I lost the election. There's so much drug activity now," he pulled his hands out of his pockets and grabbed a pitchfork. "It seemed like all we ever did was drug bust," he started to clean a stall.

Dallas followed Burt. "These are some beautiful horses. When did you get these?" He petted Prince and Duchess.

"Oh, they belong to Sierra. Raindancer is hers, too." He pointed to the horse.

"Speaking of Sierra, where is she?"

"She took James and Hope to pick up a rental car. They went home today."

"Are they her parents?"

Burt looked at him, "What do you think?"

"Well, was she adopted?"

Burt moved the wheelbarrow and ran his tongue over his teeth. "I'll let her tell you."

"Do you think she would go to a New Years' party with me?" He closed the gate to the stall.

"Ask her," he grinned as he moved the wheelbarrow.

Sierra pulled in the driveway and saw Dallas' truck. She started to breathe heavily and she felt butterflies in her stomach. Her face felt flush.

NEW BEGINNINGS

Burt mixed the formula and headed to the stall. "Well, look at that."

Dallas peered in the stall. "I have never in my life."

Pebbles and the calf were curled up together sleeping on the hay.

Sierra nervously entered the barn. "What's going on?"

Burt pointed down. Dallas looked at her, biting his bottom lip.

She looked in the stall, "That's just precious, a match made in heaven."

"Maybe you need to name the bull Precious."

She looked at Dallas. "That's a girl's name, silly." She lightly backhanded him in the stomach.

He wasn't expecting it. "Oh," he laughed and gasped for air at the same time.

The calf rose to his feet and Pebbles ran from all the attention. The calf ran to the bottle and almost knocked Burt down. He held to the bottle a little tighter. "I think we need to name him Bammer."

"How about Bam-Bam?" she looked at Dallas.

"Pebbles and Bam-Bam," Burt said.

"That's perfect," Dallas shook his head.

"I like it," Sierra said matter of factly. "Bam-Bam it is." She leaned against a post.

There was silence.

"That reminds me, there's fireworks for New Years at the

casino, you want to go?" Dallas toed the saw dust and looked at her.

She felt butterflies and smiled as she looked up at him. She looked at Burt for his approval. Burt winked at her. "Yeah, sure. I haven't been there yet."

"They have a nice restaurant, we can do dinner and go from there," he slipped his hands in his back pockets.

She bit her bottom lip and tried not to be too excited. "Okay, sounds good."

He started to walk away from Burt, his hands still in his back pockets. "Do you like to dance?"

She turned to follow him. "I love to dance, but it's been a while." She played with a strand of hair. "I may be a little rusty."

"Oh, it's like riding a horse, you never forget." He halfway turned to meet her approval. "We'll just go with the flow."

She looked at him, still playing with her hair. "Yeah, we can do that."

Dallas opened his truck door. "I brought you a little something." He reached to the back seat for a flat box with a ribbon on it.

"That's sweet. You really shouldn't have, we just met." She pulled the ribbon. "Thank you."

"It's not much," he smiled at her.

She lifted out a fluffy white robe. They both chuckled.

"I thought you could use it."

"You thought right, I threw the other one away." She bit her bottom lip. "Normally, I would have on scrubs and gowns to keep the grunge off."

"Are you a nurse or something?" he held the truck door open.

She hugged the box. "Oh, no. I'm a veterinarian."

Dallas' eyes widened and he smiled. "Really?"

"Yes, really," her eyes widened, and she smiled.

He ran his hand over his face. "I'm not believing this."

She looked at him and her tongue went across her teeth.

He watched her tongue and back to her big brown eyes. "I…have to…go. I'll call you later. I'll get your number from Burt."

"Okay, talk to you later." She waved as he got in his truck, still holding the box to her chest.

~~~~~

She went immediately to rummage through her closet. "What in the world am I going to wear?"

Burt came to her cabin and knocked, but let himself in. "Sierra, we need to talk."

"I'm looking for something to wear on my date," she held up a couple of dresses.

Burt shook his head no. "That casino is like Peyton's Place. You know you're gonna' have to be careful over there." He leaned against her bedroom door.

She was in the closet. "What are you trying to say?" She came out.

"I have no doubt you'll be in safe hands with Dallas," he stepped closer to her.

Sierra tossed some dresses on the bed.

Burt put both hands on her shoulders. "No one can know who you really are, not yet. I have informants that work in the casino."

"Tell me what I need to know, instead of beating around the bush."

"It's not that simple. Come with me, we need to take a little drive."

~~~~~

They pulled into her parents' old place.

"Why are we here?" Her voice quivered.

"I rent this place, so they always have eyes on the casino. Technically all this is yours. It put you through college and built your cabin."

They got out. "Follow me," he started walking to a storage building and unlocked it. "It's full of your mom and dad's things."

She covered her mouth and tears welled up in her eyes.

Though Burt was rugged, he had carefully packed away their things. "You might find something to wear right here," he unzipped a tall container filled with dresses and costumes.

She exhaled and smiled in surprise. "I remember this," she reached for a dress then hugged it close to her.

Sierra could see the casino over Burt's shoulder. She sniffled, "Wait, why do you have informants in the casino? You're not sheriff anymore."

"This ain't about being sheriff. Think about it, why do you think we changed your name? You said you needed answers. Why do you think I had you go live with James and Hope? Why did

James teach you to fight?"

Her voice trembled. "Are you telling me, the accident was no accident?"

"That's right baby girl," he pulled her to him and hugged her.

The tears began to stream steadily down her cheeks.

"I'll tell you what I know, but you have to be careful." They sat in the doorway and talked.

Sierra listened intensely and began to understand why all the secrecy was necessary. She squinted her big brown eyes as she looked over at the casino. She began to feel the fire ignite inside of her. She gathered up some dresses and loaded them in the truck.

~~~~~

Out on the main road, Burt pointed out Dallas' clinic. It was right next to a big building that was a concrete company.

"The same people that run the casino own the concrete company," he looked at her.

She looked at him, "That's an odd combination."

He raised his eyebrows and nodded yes. "Let's grab something to eat while we're out," he turned the truck toward a restaurant.

~~~~~

Sierra tried to stay busy and was highly anticipating her date with Dallas. She did some errands. She stopped at the dry cleaners to pick up her party dress. A white Hummer was sitting at the cleaners. It was the same woman she saw at the pizza place.

Sierra approached the counter and smiled at the woman, "Hello."

The lady behind the counter said, "Can I help you honey?"

"I need to pick up my dress."

"What's the name?"

"Sierra Wilson," she waited patiently.

"That's a pretty party dress, you must be going to the big party at the casino," she hung the dress on a hook.

"I sure am."

"Oh, I'll be there. I guess I'll see you there," a lady said in a northern accent.

Sierra turned to look at the woman behind her.

"I'm Anne Roche', like the candy," she turned abruptly to the lady at the counter, not waiting for Sierra's reply. "Have you found mine yet? I don't have all day."

"Yes, I found yours. Your name was misspelled."

"I'm not surprised, you people can't spell, and you speak this drawl language," she grabbed her attire and whirled out of the room.

Sierra and the lady watched her.

Anne looked at the truck beside her and read the sticker in the window, "Silly boys, trucks are for girls." She pouted her lips, "pppuh."

"Well, that was interesting." Sierra turned back to the woman.

"She can take her Yankee accent and attitude and go back up north for all I care," she took Sierra's money.

Sierra took the dress. "I hope your day gets better."

"She's always like that," she waved her hand in disgust.

~~~~~

Sierra stopped at the store to pick up some things. She noticed several people staring at her. She tried to hide her face behind her hood.

The lady at the register asked, "Do I know you? You remind me of somebody, but I can't quite put my finger on it yet."

"No, I just moved here. They say we all have a twin," she smiled at the lady and took her bags.

~~~~~

Johnny, Burt and Sierra were lifting heavy bags of feed from her truck.

"This is back breaking," she said. "We need to hire more help. What do you think about getting a couple of young guys that are on probation for something simple? You know, somebody that needs guidance but hasn't messed up too bad yet," she handed Burt a sack of grain.

He laid the bag down, "I'm all ears."

Johnny huffed, "Me too."

Burt and Johnny looked at her while they rested.

"Besides that, I've got some ideas about how to bring in some more money around here," she jumped down from the truck.

Burt asked, "What are you thinking?"

"Well, we've got the river. It would be easy to get white water rafting started."

"I suppose we could buy an old bus and some rafts," Burt wiped his brow. "I can talk to my buddy Beau Sammons. He's a probation officer and I can bounce the idea off of him."

Johnny added, "I think I know where an old bus is that we can get cheap. We'll have to paint it of course."

"Can we get a new sign for the ranch? That one's falling apart," she pointed toward the entrance.

"You don't have to ask sweetheart. You own half of this ranch." Burt hoisted the bag again and grinned at her.

"Awesome! Right now, I'm going to get ready for my date. It's going to be a great New Year!"

She pranced out of the barn. Her phone rang, "Hello."

"Hey, it's Dallas. I've had a slight emergency. I'm running about an hour behind."

"That's okay," she continued to walk to her cabin.

"Can I meet you at the bar inside the casino?"

"Sure, that's not a problem. Thanks for letting me know."

"Okay, looking forward to seeing you."

"See you soon," she smiled and thought, now I'll have time to curl my hair.

About an hour and a half later, Burt and Johnny knocked on her door. "Are you 'bout ready yet? We want to see you all dressed up."

She opened the door.

"Wow."

Johnny whistled. "You're gonna' knock their socks off, girl."

"You're beautiful. Dallas won't believe his eyes when he sees you," Burt kissed her cheek.

"Thanks guys."

~~~~~

Sierra let the valet take her car and she nervously walked inside. She showed her license to the guard, "This place is big. Where is the bar?"

"Go downstairs, it's right in the center," the guard said.

"Thanks," she put away her license.

A lot of heads turned her way.

She made her way through the crowd confidently and thought, 'I hope Dallas comes soon,' and smiled.

A lot of people were dressed in tuxes and fancy dresses.

Sierra entered the bar area. She looked over the crowd and when her eyes met Dallas' she smiled and exhaled with relief to see him sooner than later.

He smiled at her and walked toward her. "You are absolutely stunning," he picked up her hand and kissed it. He twirled her around and guided her hand over her head.

Her hair was curled and hung down in the back. It was pulled away from her face with strands curled and hanging down the sides of her face.

The dress had a tightly fitted bodice and see through lace on the sleeves. The skirt was loosely flowing and gave a glimpse to her shapely legs. Her sparkling shoes added height to her slender frame.

"I just want to stand and look at you," he smiled.

"You're stunning yourself in that tux, turn around," she circled her hand.

He did some smooth dance moves and turned around. He finished by running his hand over his hair.

She licked her finger and stuck it to him. "Sssss, you're hot."

"Shall we go to dinner?" he offered her his arm.

She slid her hand in his elbow. "We shall. I'm starving."

~~~~~

They entered the restaurant. "Reservation for Davenport." They were taken to their candlelit table with a red tablecloth. He pulled the chair out for her.

"Thank you," she sat down. "Why did you shave? You look different."

"It'll grow back in a couple of days."

"I like it either way, it's nice."

"Thanks, now order anything you want, okay?"

The conversation came easy and flowed naturally, as if they had known each other for a very long time and they laughed.

"Hey, what time is it?" he looked at his watch. "They're supposed to make some big announcement at 10:00. We need to go to the ballroom," they stood, and he held her hand as they walked.

~~~~~

They entered the ballroom and once again, all heads turned their way.

"Do you see all these people staring at me?" he said. "Is my hair sticking up?" he ran his fingers through his black tousled hair. "Is my coat in my pants?" he reached behind. "Is there tissue paper stuck to my shoes?" he looked at each shoe. "If there is we're just going to have to leave. I'll be too embarrassed to stay."

She laughed at him and covered her mouth.

He chuckled at himself.

A man approached Dallas and punched his arm playfully. "You better behave yourself, I can tell you're up to no good."

They shook hands and laughed.

"How could you guess? Hey, I want you to meet someone. This is Sierra. This is Jesse and Ellie Woods."

Sierra put her hand out, "Nice to meet you both."

"Likewise," Jesse said, and Ellie gave her a nod and a smile.

"Jenna, my sister, is trying to find us a table," he looked around. "Would you two care to join us?"

Dallas looked at Sierra and they both nodded in agreement.

"Sure," Dallas replied.

Ellie said, "I see her over there waving," she pointed, "she must have found us a table."

They all started to go toward Jenna making their way through the crowded room.

After introductions were made, Sierra looked around and asked Jenna, "Do you know where the restroom is?"

Jenna pointed, "It's over there and down the hallway."

Sierra's eye caught Anne Roche'. She caught Jenna's eye as well. "I bet that dress cost ten grand."

"Well, she should have spent some of it on her hair, it looks like she stuck her finger in an electric socket," Sierra replied.

The whole table laughed.

At 10:00pm, Anne Roche' asked, "May I have your attention please. This is Alan Dabadee and Carlos Cilia." Some Chinese men were there, too.

Sierra made her way to the front and took pictures. She zoomed up close for each one.

Anne noticed Sierra but liked the attention.

Mr. Dabadee announced plans for ski slopes with construction starting in the spring. The audience clapped and cheered. Sierra made her way back to the table.

They had served everyone with champagne. Mr. Dabadee and his crew held up a glass, "I propose a toast, to new beginnings!"

Sierra and Dallas had their own reasons to toast to new beginnings and clinked their glasses together. They looked in each other's eyes, as they sipped. Music began to play again.

Dallas held out his hand. "Will you dance with me?" as he stood.

She placed her hand in his and followed him to the dance floor. It was a slow dance.

He rested his hand in the small of her back and held her other hand ever so gently.

The music seemed to fade away and it felt like they were the only two people in the room.

He pulled her closer and held her hand tighter.

She felt the muscles in his shoulders and arms and held him tighter.

They looked in each other's' eyes and exhaled. Their hearts were beating like thunder.

He pulled her closer. She did not resist. He could feel her every breath as they stepped to the beat, it felt as if a force field pulled them closer together and they could not resist it.

She felt completely safe.

Dallas pressed his cheek to hers and slid his hand up her back to pull her against him. He whispered, "You are so beautiful."

She held him tighter. When the music changed to a higher beat they didn't even seem to notice.

Then he kissed her behind the ear and led her off the dance floor.

At their table, he took off his coat. "I'll be right back, don't go anywhere," he wiped his brow.

"I'll be here," she sat down and felt dizzy and shaky. She sipped some champagne to calm her nerves. She wondered, 'Did he feel the same way she did. Surely, he must, I could see it in his eyes and feel it in his touch.' She smiled.

Dallas returned and said, "Are you ready for more? I had to cool down for a minute."

She looked up at him and smiled. She lifted up her hand for him to take it in his.

He led her to the dance floor, and they danced and danced.

"I need to rest a minute; I'm not used to these heels. I'll be right back, okay?"

"Okay, but hurry because I don't want to take my eyes off of you," he winked at her.

When she returned, Dallas had gotten them some water to have at the table and he was outside again to cool off.

Sierra looked at Ellie and the two smiled.

Ellie said, "It feels good to be in love, doesn't it?"

"Oh, it's just our first date."

Ellie and Jenna looked surprised.

"You could have fooled me," Ellie said. Jenna replied, "Y'all make a nice couple."

"Thanks," Sierra bit her bottom lip.

Anne was making her way through the crowd. She stopped at tables to talk to party goers. She came and sat down by Ellie with her back to Sierra.

"I am so glad you came, Ellie. We are going to have an awesome firework display so make sure to stay, okay? It's too bad your father, the senator couldn't make it."

"Sure," Ellie smiled and shook her head. "My father stays out of town a lot, I'm certain that he would love to be here."

Sierra got something out of her purse. Anne was standing behind Sierra but didn't speak to her. Sierra turned and squirted something on Anne's dress. Immediately, there was a foul odor. Ellie and Jenna saw Sierra do it.

Sierra put her fingers to her lips, "Shhh, a little payback."

The guys returned to the table and brought three other guys with them.

"Look who we found, Travis, Taylor and Tyler," Dallas said.

Jesse said, "Y'all know my wife Ellie, sister Jenna, and this is Sierra."

The girls waved.

Tyler poked his elbow in Taylor's ribs, "That's Ms. Cherokee," half whispered.

Dallas asked, "What's that horrible smell?"

Jesse scratched his head, "Smells like fox pee."

Dallas looked puzzled, "Or somebody has on some really bad cologne, Travis is that you?"

"It's not me. The smeller must be the fellow. Who wants to dance?" Travis pulled Jenna to her feet and led them to the dance floor.

Jesse and Ellie were in front of Dallas and Sierra.

Ellie turned to Sierra and said, "I think that dress was Armani."

"Well now it's a stinky Armani."

They giggled and watched Anne make her way through the crowd and the reaction people gave her. Every time the girls looked at one another they would start to giggle.

Dallas said, "Why are you girls so giddy?"

"I'll tell you later, I promise," as she giggled.

"I think you ladies are up to something. Hey, this is good music for the salsa. Do you know it?"

"I don't know if I remember."

"You are not rusty, you got this."

They twirled around the dance floor and didn't notice that people moved to give them the floor.

Someone in the crowd said, "They look like a match made in heaven." When the song finished, Dallas dipped her and looked her face to face.

The crowd clapped.

Travis yelled, "Kiss her Dallas."

He looked in her eyes and brought her upright. He led her off the floor and they waved to the crowd.

"It's going to be midnight soon," Dallas put on his jacket.

She looked in his eyes, "I don't want tonight to end."

He took her hand, "Me either." He led her to the patio.

She shivered, "Brrr, it got cold."

Dallas wrapped his arms around her inside his coat and held her close. When the countdown began, he turned Sierra around to look in her eyes. She put her arms around his waist underneath the jacket. He slid his hands around her neck underneath her hair.

They could feel each other breathing and looked at each other. When their lips touched, there were fireworks behind closed eyes. She knew in that moment her life would be forever changed.

Travis, Taylor, and Tyler walked by them.

Travis said, "Get a room."

Dallas and Sierra heard nothing but their own heartbeats and the energy that surged between them.

Little did anyone know that Anne was on a balcony alone. She looked down at the happy couple and turned up her drink. She disappeared into the dark.

Dallas took Sierra's hand, "Let's get you inside. You're shaking."

She fanned her face with her hand and thought, 'I'm not cold, it was that kiss."

TIMING IS EVERYTHING

Dallas followed Sierra to make sure she got home safely.

She shivered standing by her car, "It's too cold to stand out here, would you like to come in?"

"Just a minute maybe."

~~~~~

"The fire will get us warm quick," she kicked her shoes off by the door. She turned on the fire logs. "If you want something to drink, help yourself to the fridge."

"I'll just get some water; do you want some?" he walked toward the kitchen.

"Please. I'm just going to change really quick," she went toward the bedroom.

Moments later when she returned, she said, "Oh this is much more comfy. I hope you don't mind," she had slipped on flannel PJ's and her white robe.

"I don't mind, after all I've already seen you in your PJ's." They both laughed, and he handed her some water.

"Yes, you have," she took a sip.

"I'm glad the robe fits."

"Me too. It's warm for these cold nights to cuddle up and watch TV. Thank you again and thank you for a wonderful night," she glanced away from his eyes to look into the fire light.

"I had a really good time tonight," he played with her hair. "I never go out like that."

"Me too…a good time, I mean," she stammered. "I don't go

out drinking either."

"I like to keep my wits about me," he took her water and sat both glasses on a table.

"I know what you mean, I didn't want to forget...anything about tonight."

He placed his hands underneath her hair and looked at her.

Their hearts raced. She licked her lips and looked at his. He pulled her to him and they kissed passionately. She ran her fingers through his hair.

"I think I better go," he looked in her eyes.

"Um, that's probably a good idea. I hope we can see each other again," she suggested.

"Yeah, absolutely," he squeezed her hand and led her to the door. He opened the door, but turned and kissed her passionately again.

"You really should go," she said, breathing deeply.

"I know, I'm going, I'm gone." Their hands slipped apart.

Burt was getting out of his truck and waved at them.

~~~~~

Sierra watched the clock and tossed and turned most of the night. She recalled every minute she could and all the different feelings she had experienced. What was it about this man that made him so attractive and desirable? She prayed, "Thank you, Lord, for all the wonderful blessings you've given me and for making Dallas a part of my life." It was early morning when she finally drifted off to sleep.

~~~~~

Sierra made her appearance at the barn after lunch time.

"Good afternoon," Burt said. "You look like you had a good time last night, you're glowing."

"I had a wonderful time," she smiled and leaned against a stall door. "He's Mr. Dreamy McSteamy." She fanned her face, "He's such a gentleman, he can dance, he's funny and he's...HOT," her eyes got big. "Seriously, there's something different about him."

"You like him, huh?"

"You think," she ran her hand down her neck. "Everybody in town must know him."

Burt watered the horses, "Well have you thought about being a little harder to get?"

"No way, what, like you?" she moved the hose. "I don't want

to be an old maid. When a good one comes along, you better hold on tight. And where were you last night?"

"Nunya."

Where's Nunya?"

"Nunya business," he smirked out one side of his mouth and looked from under the brim of his hat.

Her phone rang, she pointed her finger at him. "Hello."

"Hey, it's Bobbie. Happy New Year."

"Happy New Year to you."

"Are you getting settled in?"

"Yeah, it's going great. You'll have to come visit."

"I'll have to do that. Well good. I hate to have to break some bad news to you. I just wanted to let you know Dr. Vargas passed away."

"What?"

"He killed himself. I guess it was worse than we thought."

"Oh no," she covered her mouth with her hand.

"He lost everything, he just gave up."

"That's a shame. He had no faith at all. He was a good person deep down. It's so hard to believe."

"Yes, it is...well keep in touch. I have to call some of the others."

"I will, thanks for letting me know," she looked out over the pasture for a minute.

"What's wrong?" Burt had noticed her demeanor changed.

"My old boss killed himself. I'm just thinking how sad when so many things happen to us. I realize we are in control of absolutely nothing," she turned to look at him.

"You are so right, baby girl," he turned to leave and stopped. "Hey, tomorrow I'm going to talk to Beau about the probey's. Johnny has gone to check out an old bus."

"Okay," she nodded.

~~~~~

Over the mountain a car pulled off the road and set out a tricolor beagle puppy.

"Good luck, little fella."

He whimpered and watched the car go down the road. He laid down on the edge of the road in the leaves to wait for them to return.

~~~~~

Sierra turned the calf out into the arena. He went running and jumping. Another calf and his mother were also in the arena. The two calves played and butted their heads together.

Sierra stood there and watched.

The mother didn't seem to mind the other calf and even let it nurse her. Sierra clasped her fingers to her chin. She moved closer as they played. Her outback coat flapped in the breeze as she twirled around and played with them. Her hair floated as she turned.

A mysterious man watched her, his arms rested on the fence. His face covered from the shadow of a cowboy hat. He had on an outback coat and cowboy hat. He propped one foot on the lowest board of the fence.

"I hope my dad would be proud that I saved your life, Bam-Bam. I wish he could see you."

She heard a high-pitched whistle and turned toward the man at the fence. She started to walk toward him. "I wonder who that is?" The closer she got, the more he looked down and his hat covered his face. "Can I help you?"

No answer.

She continued curiously and kept her eye on the hat. She stopped just shy of him. "Can I help you?" She was almost annoyed.

The man slowly lifted his head and revealed and unshaven face and sheepish grin. Big blue eyes looked up from underneath the brim of the hat. Dallas and Sierra's eyes met, she began to smile.

Sierra did not know that Bam-Bam had followed her, and he butted her straight into Dallas' arms and face to face.

They both started laughing.

She tipped back his hat, "Hello cowboy."

He stepped higher on the fence and leaned over to give her a kiss. "I hope it's alright that I stopped by without calling first."

She shook her head yes and bit her bottom lip.

"You look like you're dancing with the cows now. What are you doing?" He climbed over the fence.

"Well, that's it, I'm dancing with the cows now." They walked toward the calf, as they laughed.

"Did you forget to shave today?"

"Nah, just feeling tough, decided to look the part," he poked out his chest and tried to walk bow legged.

She giggled, "Where's your chew?"
He poked his tongue behind his lip and pretended to spit, "Got that covered, little lady. How's Bam-Bam?"
"I put him in here hoping the mama would let him nurse and she did some. I'll just have to see how it goes."
"That's good thinking, you might make a cattle woman yet."
She grabbed his hat and put it on. "You think so?" as she backed away.
"I think it looks better on you," he stepped toward her and reached for the hat.
She turned to run, "Betcha' can't get it back."
He chased after her. She slid under the fence, like sliding over home plate, and ran toward the barn. He climbed over the fence and went after her.
She scurried up the ladder to the loft and pulled off her coat. He got to the loft but, she grabbed the pulley for lifting hay, and she slipped back down to the bottom. Dallas had to come down the ladder again so, he pulled his coat off and laid it with hers.
Sierra hid on one side of Raindancer. She held to his mane and wrapped his tail around her foot. Dallas looked straight at Raindancer and didn't see her. When the coast was clear, she got on Raindancer's back and lifted herself through a hole used to push hay down from the loft.
Dallas came back in the stable and he could see dust particles falling in the rays of the setting sun.
He knew she was up top. He crept up the ladder again.
"Atchew!" Sierra couldn't hold back the sneeze.
"I know you're up here," Dallas said.
She slid around some hay to dodge him and reached a loft door. Then she used a rope to repel down. "Do you give up," she yelled from down below.
"Not on your life," he stood at the loft door.
She made her way back to Rain-dancer and got on his back again and back up to the loft. She stuck her head down the hole and looked for him but did not see him anywhere. "Do you give up?" She locked the latch door and sat quietly, listening.
Suddenly he pounced on her, knocking her into the loose hay. "I got you this time," he pinned her down.
They started laughing. He gazed into her eyes and held her arms down.

51

She tried to get away, "Next time I won't let you win."

"Let me? I still got you," he stretched her arms upward to get closer to her face. "Betcha' can't get loose."

She raised her eyebrows. "Well, I don't want to hurt you. I could get loose if I wanted to," half whispered. She felt her heart flutter and her temperature rise.

They looked deep in each other's eyes.

Dallas barely kissed her nose, her cheeks, and pulled away twice before he kissed her open lips. He slowly kissed down her neck, she moaned, he held one arm over her head. Their fingers laced together, and he slid one hand to her back. He rolled her on top of him.

She kissed his neck and chest. Chill bumps covered his body.

He pulled her upward until their lips met. Her hair fell around his face, and he played with her hair, his thumb caressed her cheek.

She ran her fingers through his hair and around his unshaven jawline and across his lips. He kissed her fingers as they looked into each other's eyes.

It started to get dark. "Let me show you something," she rolled to the side and opened a loft door.

It was one of the most beautiful sunsets over the mountains they had ever seen. Every color of pinks and oranges faded into the nighttime blues. They held each other close and watched as the sun drew the last ounce of breath from its day.

She turned to sit cross legged. "Can you teach me how to whistle like you did earlier?"

"I…don't…know. That takes special skills," he stuck a straw in his mouth.

She puckered her lips, but no sound came out. "Come on, show me," she pleaded.

"There's a couple ways you could do it," he put his hands behind his head. "You gotta' move your tongue a certain way," the straw bobbed up and down.

"Show me what to do with my tongue," she waited.

"You gotta' do tongue curls and stuff,". he chuckled.

She started to move her tongue under her lip and across her teeth. She knew he was playing her, "You mean like this?" she teased him.

He watched her tongue intensely. "More." He grinned and his breathing increased.

She continued to play him and watched him. "You liar," she shook her head and grabbed his ribs to tickle him.

He laughed and grabbed her again, pinning her to the hay. "You have a good poker face."

She grunted, trying to get away and wiggled underneath his body. She tried to puff her hair out of her face.

"Shhh," he held her arms down and used his face to move her hair. He let go of her arms and cradled her neck with one arm. Her breathing intensified as he slowly and lightly kissed her face. She could feel his muscular body as she clung to his back. She pulled her leg up, which he greeted with his hand on her thigh. She moaned with pleasure as he slid his hands to her buttock. He pressed his open lips to hers and pulled her pelvis into him as his tongue ran across her teeth and underneath her lip. They both gasped for air. He touched his forehead to hers and opened his eyes.

"Lord, have mercy," he whispered. "Don't worry I respect you."

"Don't worry I can tell you are not like other guys."

"I just keep asking myself if you are for real."

"Let me assure you, I am very real."

DECISIONS

Dallas took a deep breath. "I'm going home to take another cold shower."

She giggled.

He got to his feet and pulled her to hers. "You think that's funny?"

"Yeah," she held his hand as they walked across the loft.

"Torture." He climbed down the ladder.

She climbed down and turned to him before she got to the bottom.

He held her off the ground. "It's pure torture." He put her down. "You drive me crazy, you know that right," as he looked up in to her big brown eyes.

"Do I now," she cocked her head and grinned at him. "Well maybe we could go riding next time," she suggested.

"Sounds good. Where's everybody at anyway?"

"Johnny went to Snowbird to check out a bus so this summer we can start rafting," they walked to his truck. "Burt's probably in Nunya."

He looked puzzled.

"This place needs some work, plus I've got some good ideas how to bring in more money. I'm just trying to help Burt out, you know."

"Sounds interesting. If you have time tomorrow, why don't you stop by the clinic, and we can have some lunch." He kissed her forehead before getting in his truck.

She waved and blew him a kiss. "Okay."

~~~~~

She put the cows in the barn. Pebbles was laying in the hay waiting for Bam-Bam. Diesel followed Sierra everywhere she went. She bent over to pet him. "You're looking good, Diesel. I feel your hair coming back." He wagged his tail and licked her face. Sierra puckered her lips and tried to whistle all the way to the cabin.

~~~~~

Across the mountain, a beagle puppy scrounged for food and warmth. Occasionally, he got lucky, and someone tossed him a morsel. He was scared and cold when he crawled underneath an old house.

~~~~~

Sierra woke before dawn and tended to the animals. She fed Bam-Bam with the bottle to make sure he was getting enough nutrition. She put the cows out to pasture. The horses were let out to graze in the lower pasture. She noticed the fencing needed some work. She saddled Duke for a short ride. Burt and Johnny made their way to the barn.

"Why are you up so early little lady," asked Johnny.

"Lots to do today."

"Are you sure you can handle Duke," Burt asked.

"Of course, why would I not be able to Burt. You know me better than anybody. I can't believe you would even say that" she rubbed her face with the back of her hand.

"Nobody has been able to ride him without him constantly rearing up. That's how he got his name. He's like his daddy. He was ornery as hell to break. He damn near killed us."

Johnny shook his head in agreement.

"Like father, like son, huh," she put a foot in the stirrup and hiked up into the saddle. She looked at her watch. "I'll be back in three hours. If not," Duke was anxiously stomping around, "I'm going up there." She pointed toward the mountain and nudged the horse's ribs with her heel. Duke started to trot and then broke into a run. Sierra's hair blew in the wind. She pushed Dallas' hat further down on her head. He ran until he got to a steep hill, then he slowed down on his own. She looked down on the ranch and then back up the trail. 'It has been too darn long.' She felt so free. "I am so blessed."

~~~~~

At the top, she could see for miles. She looked down on her parent's old place. It was very rocky on one side of the mountain, and a sharp edge of stone stuck upward. That's why it was named Lucifer's Ridge. The end of the ridge was higher. It was called the Devil's Courthouse. The river ran through the canyon and a large waterfall cascaded down through the canyon. The river ran through the ranch. She got down to walk a while. "Duke, I forgot how beautiful it is up here." She stared out at the layers of blue and purples, fog ran between some layers of the mountains. "It's so peaceful. I know one thing, I sure don't miss the city." She looked down at the casino and Dallas' clinic. She took off his hat and closed her eyes to smell it. "Mmm, I could eat him up," and she bit the hat. Duke softly muzzled against her ear, as if to wake her up and come on. "What, I can't help it. Don't tell him, okay?" She put the hat back on. Duke neighed as if making a pact with her. Sierra looked at the time, it was 11:11. "We better get back down there, don't need a search party coming after us." She mounted Duke. Duke reared up, his hooves pawed at the wind.

~~~~~

Back in the valley, Duke broke into a run. She knew he would head straight for the barn, so she made him go past it. "You gotta' learn who's boss, Duke." Burt and Johnny watched as she flew by. A car was coming up the driveway. Duke and Sierra ran past the car. Two guys inside turned around to watch her. Sierra turned Duke around to head back to the barn. The car parked, and Beau and two other guys got out. Duke ran toward the men. Sierra reigned him in and he stopped just in time, but she got off before he completely halted.

Beau introduced Dylan and Landyn, identical twins.

"Nice riding," Dylan said, and both guys came over to pet the horse. Another vehicle came down the road, followed by a bus. It was an ugly green color.

Sierra looked at her watch. "Burt, will you show Dylan and Landyn to their cabin?" She looked at Johnny. "Will you get some baby blue paint for the bus? We need barbed wire, too. Dylan and Landyn can kerry the horses while you get the paint," she led Duke into the barn and began to pull off the saddle. "Guys, come here." She gave the saddle to one of them. "The tack room is over there," she pointed. "Make yourselves at home, this is a busy place. How can I tell which one is which?" She looked at each one back and forth.

"Landyn has a birthmark on the back of his neck," Dylan pointed to his neck.

Landyn slapped his hand away.

"Okay then." She started to walk away. "Oh, there's three more horses out in the lower pasture.

Burt and Johnny will show you." She got in her car and left.

The men stood there letting their orders sink in. Johnny said, "I told you a storm was coming."

They all looked up in the sky, bewildered.

~~~~~

The beagle pup began his journey over the mountain. He smelled something he had never smelled before.

~~~~~

In town, the sheriff made a phone call. "Just letting you know something is going on over there."

"Thanks."

~~~~~

Sierra pulled into Dallas' clinic. She noticed the chain link fence and layers of barbed wire at the top going around the plant. 'That is so odd especially for this little town,' she thought. She slipped into the clinic, not knowing what to expect. "Hello." Someone was singing. She went down the hall. She stood at the doorway. She watched Dallas looking for something. He had on black scrubs, and he was singing.

When he turned around, he was startled to see her. He made a smooth recovery and started to sing. "Hello darling, why are you sneaking around?" He walked toward her.

"I'm not sneaking." She smiled and stepped toward him.

He wrapped his arms around her, picking her up. "I sent Emily to get us some lunch." He began to dance around the room with her.

"You did? I'm hungry. I forgot to eat breakfast I was so busy."

He lowered her to the floor and held her hand. "Let me show you around." He led her to a break room and gave her a cold Mountain Dew.

They continued to walk around through the clinic, and he held her hand.

"It's nice I like it."

"Trip, I have lunch." A voice called out.

Dallas answered, "We are in here."

A lady came in the break room and sat a bag down.

"Emily, this is the lady I've been telling you about."

"Nice to meet you, Emily. I'm Sierra." She put out her hand.

Emily smiled at her and reached for her hand. "Nice to meet you, Trip has told me about you." she took a sandwich and left the room.

"Why did she call you Trip?" she pulled out a burger.

"Three D's," he pointed to his scrub's logo, "Dr. Dallas Davenport." He unwrapped a burger.

"I like that." She took a bite.

"Why were you so busy this morning?" he said, taking a bite.

"Just getting things going over there. I took Duke to the top of the mountain." She chugged down some Dew. "I can see your clinic from the top." She covered her mouth.

"I'd like to see that. Maybe Saturday I can bring my horses over. They need to be ridden."

"Yeah, that sounds like fun."

"This is a good burger. Do you want some fries?" he held one up to her mouth.

She took a bite. "It is a good burger. Fries, too." She burped. "Excuse me," and they laughed.

"Slow down, you're inhaling it."

She looked at her watch and pointed. "I've got to meet somebody, two actually. The bank and a construction company."

"Oh yeah?" he looked at her.

She nodded.

"You are busy."

"Burt really needs my help to get things going again."

"Okay, I'm sure he appreciates it."

"Well, thanks for lunch and the tour." She stood up.

He walked her to the car, he cupped his hands around her face and lightly kissed her lips.

"I'll see you soon," she got in her car.

"You can bet on it," he waved.

~~~~~

"Hey, Mr. Colton. How are you," Sierra asked standing in the doorway of his office.

The man stood up to greet her. "Doing well, and yourself?"

"I'm fine, thank you. I need to transfer a large sum of money to this account." She handed him a piece of paper.

"Come in dear and have a seat."

His eyes got big when he looked at her account. "That's a lot of money, young lady."

"Yes, sir it is." She nodded.

As soon as she left the office, she called Triple T construction. "Hey, I'm running a little late. I'll be there in about fifteen minutes. Can you wait?"

~~~~~

She pulled in at the ranch and there sat Travis, Taylor, and Tyler.

"Hey, that's Ms. Cherokee," Tyler said.

"Her name is Sierra. That's Dallas' girl." Travis said, "So mind your manners."

Sierra got out of her car holding some rolled-up paper, "I'm surprised to see you all. I had no idea that Triple T Construction was you guys."

"Really. You just randomly picked us?"

"Yeah, I did. Weird, huh?"

"I'll say," Travis said.

"And Dallas is really your uncle?" she asked.

"I swear," Travis put up his hand.

"I have big plans for this place, shall we get started?"

The three guys gathered around her, and she began to unroll the paper across her car hood.

~~~~~

At dinner, Burt and Sierra discussed her ideas. Burt was all in.

"How do the new guys seem to be? Did they get settled?" She cleaned the table.

"Yeah, I think they'll be good for this place. They both love horses and adventure."

"Maybe I can spend some time with them tomorrow. Oh, Dallas is coming Saturday to ride."

"You two seem to be pretty smitten with each other," he leaned back in his chair.

She shook her head yes and raised her eyebrows. "He's sooo hot." She put her hands to her head and sat down again. "I feel like I have known him forever. It just feels right, you know what I'm saying."

"He's a good guy. I'm happy for you both." He shook his

head and grinned, and hesitated. "I'm pretty smitten with someone myself."

"What," she leaned forward. "You've been holding out on me, Burt Cleveland. Spill it now." She slapped his leg.

He rubbed his nose and laughed. "We've been seeing each other over a year now. Her name is Beth, she used to be my secretary. She's coming over to meet you Saturday," he rubbed his head.

"Hey, we can all go riding together. That'll be fun." She got up and smacked the back of his head. "I'm not believing you. I'm going to have to watch you, Mr. Sweet and Innocent."

He laughed.

"Does she know who I really am?"

"Yeah, she does."

~~~~~

The next day was rainy. "Osda sunalei, that means good morning in Cherokee," Sierra said, when she entered the barn to find Dylan and Landyn waiting.

"What's so good about it, it's cold and raining," Landyn said as he scraped some mud from his boot.

Sierra walked over to pet the painted horse, "This is Raindancer, guys. If you'll saddle him, I'll show you why I call him that."

"Sure, we can do that," and Dylan began to open the gate.

She double checked everything behind them.

"I told you we could do it," Landyn said.

"Just making sure. You can never be too safe." She walked over and turned on some tunes over the PA system.

"I don't see the point. It's raining so much."

"Well, he loves the rain," she mounted him and went into the arena. They lapped it a couple of times and then she guided him to the center. Raindancer began to step to the music in the rain. The guys watched in amazement. Sierra looked up to see someone talking to Burt on his porch. She decided she needed to go and investigate so she left the arena. She handed Dylan the reigns. "See, a little rain doesn't stop the show." She headed toward Burt's cabin.

The two men had on long trench coats. Her hair was soaking wet, and rain dripped from her hat and coat. She met the men on the way to their car. They looked at her awkwardly from underneath their umbrellas. She reached the porch. "Who's that?"

Burt stuffed his hands in his pockets. "Casino people."

"What do they want?" She looked at him.

"To meet," he hesitated and looked at her with a frown, "land."

"So, what did you tell "em?"

"They would get and answer Saturday."

"We have an appointment Wednesday with Mr. Wesley to put my name on everything."

"Yeah, we have to get that done. Here's what we're gonna' do Saturday," he grinned and cut his eyes toward her.

~~~~~

That night, Sierra had many thoughts and unanswered questions that tumbled around in her head like shards of glass. She looked over at the clock, it was 11:11. When she finally went to sleep, she dreamed of the bull again.

She woke suddenly and got out of bed to get a drink of water. She looked out the window to see some animals run between the cabins. She couldn't make out what they were. She went back to bed unconcerned, until she heard the horses neighing loudly and kicking the stalls, her feet hit the floor. She grabbed her 9mm pistol from the nightstand, and burst out the door barefooted. She headed cautiously into the barn where she came face to face with glowing eyes and gnarly teeth. Growling came from behind her as well. She shot the animal in front of her killing him instantly. The one behind her ran for the hills. She could see a few of them in the moonlight. Diesel charged after them. "No, Diesel, come back!"

Burt rushed down to the barn.

"Are you alright? What the hell is going on?"

She shook like a leaf in the wind. "Yeah." She walked back in the barn.

Johnny, Dylan, and Landyn heard the gunshot and also came running.

She stood over the coyote and panted for breath, "I've never taken an animal's spirit before."

"It's okay, we are the protectors," Johnny said. "Sometimes you have to."

"He's huge." Dylan said, standing next to her.

"They're going in heat, everybody is going to have to watch out," Johnny said.

"Are all the animals okay?" Burt started to look over each one.

Diesel came around the corner. He stood over the dead animal and sniffed at it, followed by a vicious growl.

Sierra started back to her cabin and looked over her shoulder. "Make sure these doors get shut at night. That's everybody's responsibility!"

The coyotes howled.

BUILDING BRIDGES

No one could go back to sleep after the early morning ordeal, so work began early. Johnny took the track hoe and buried the animal at the edge of the woods. The twins helped.

Sierra cooked a big breakfast for everyone. "Thanks guys, for all you do around here. Take care of me and I'll take care of you."

Dylan said, "Mama used to say I'll walk through fire for you."

"That's a powerful thought. She must really love you guys. I like that, I'll have to remember that one."

"She does. Thanks for breakfast," they got up from the table.

"You guys can take the afternoon off since it's Saturday. We have a ride planned up the mountain this afternoon," she started to clear the table.

Burt stood up and looked at Sierra. "Beth's bringing salmon to cook on the grill. You won't have to worry about dinner tonight."

"Where did she get salmon?" She carried some dishes to the kitchen.

"Her brother goes to Alaska fishing every year and brings it back." Burt followed her with his coffee cup.

She looked at Burt, "I would love to go back up there, but I don't want to go by myself. Do you remember that time we went?" She ran some dish water.

"Of course, we had a blast. All of our trips were a blast." He sipped his coffee.

"What was the name of that place that we went to?"

"Prince of Wales Island," he sat his cup down on the counter.

"Oh yeah, that guy and his family were from North Carolina. We stayed in one of their cabins."

Burt turned to leave, 'That's right, they were such a nice family. I would love to go back too."

"Hey Burt, tell the guys to leave the animals in the barn today."

"Will do." He went out the door.

~~~~~

Sierra nervously anticipated the future events of the day. She put on some makeup and French braided her hair. She looked in the mirror and tried her best to whistle, disappointed that no sound came out. She decided to tuck her jean legs into her moccasin boots. The boots had fur to keep her warm, and her coat matched. She walked to the fireplace and took down her hickory bow and quiver filled with arrows. She switched the string on the bow into the firing position and then placed them over her shoulder.

Dallas knocked on the door. "Anybody home?"

"Come on in," she turned to look toward the door.

He opened the door and much to his surprise, there stood a warrior princess.

"I didn't know we were going hunting today." He stood there looking at her.

She came and greeted him with a kiss. "We're not going hunting, I'm just being prepared." She told him what happened with the coyotes.

"I have a pistol in the truck. I'll make sure to put it on, just in case." He wrapped his arms around her.

"That's a good idea. I'm sure Burt will have his too."

"I'm glad the coyote didn't eat you up, but I couldn't blame him if he did."

She pulled her head back and looked at him puzzled.

"I've thought about it myself, a time or two."

She pinched his waist, and he laughed as he wiggled away and out the door.

~~~~~

Outside, Johnny unloaded Dallas' quarter horses. They were black with some white markings.

"This one is Comet," he patted the horse's hip, "and this one is Moonstruck," he said as he reached for the reigns.

Both horses came over to Sierra to greet her. "Siyo" (Hello) she rubbed their noses.

"I've never seen them do that before." Dallas looked on. "What did you just say."

"It means hello. Oh, did you bring what I asked for?" She hung her quiver over the saddle horn.

"I sure did, it's in the saddle bag," he placed the gun in his belt. He walked over to her and slipped something in her pocket. "Here's you a key to the clinic if you ever need anything."

Burt and Beth came out of his cabin. Burt had a pistol in his belt, he did most of the time anyway. When Beth approached Sierra, she hugged her. "For the longest time, I thought you were Burt's girlfriend," she whispered. Both of them laughed.

"Burt told me what happened this morning. I'm glad you're okay," her hand rested on Sierra's shoulder.

"It was pretty scary," she held to Comet's reigns. "I didn't have time to think about it. When it was all over with was when I started to tremble."

Johnny had saddled Prince and Duchess for Burt and Beth. He led them over to the couple and gave them the reigns.

"These are my horses. They like to stay together, side by side, but they ride good." She petted both of them.

Everyone mounted their horse.

Burt asked, "So are we ready then."

"Ready, let's go," Sierra took the lead toward the trail. "Why do you call this one Comet?"

"When he runs, the white on his legs looks like a comet. He's beautiful in an open field."

~~~~~

Conversation continued up the mountain. Once on top, they dismounted to rest and eat lunch.

Dallas started singing to Sierra as they sat around on some big rocks.

Beth whispered to Burt, "He's crazy about her, both of them are glowing."

"Do you really think so?"

"Oh yeah, honey. Just look at them."

Sierra smiled at Burt and Beth and turned to Dallas. She stood and reached for his hand and pulled him to his feet. "Look that's your clinic," she pointed it out to him.

"It sure is, but it looks so tiny from up here." They walked around, and Dallas looked over the edge of Devil's Courthouse. "This looks like a good place to repel down from. Have you ever done that?"

"No, I'm really scared of heights." She stayed away from the edge.

"It's fun, you don't have to look down." Dallas tried to convince her.

She reached for his hand, "Look, there's the casino." She pointed and pulled at him in the other direction.

"That's a nice spread. I like that big farmhouse," he pointed.

She looked at the farmhouse. "It's too big." Sierra said nothing about it being hers.

"Not if you have lots of kids," Dallas replied.

She wrapped her arms around him. "Do you want kids some day?"

He held her. "Someday."

"Yeah? How many?"

He pulled her closer and kissed her.

She pulled away slightly, "You're avoiding my question. How many?"

He licked his lips as he looked at hers. "It depends."

"What kind of answer is that?" She bit her lip.

"I'm from a big family. It was fun growing up."

"So, you want a big family?"

"Maybe."

Burt chimed in, "Hey looks like lightening has hit this tree. Sierra did you know that when you were little, there was a bad storm. Your mom got a feeling to get you out of the bathtub. She didn't get your feet on the floor when lightning struck. She said she could hear water sizzle in the tub, I guess the lightning ran through the pipes."

"Wow, that was your guardian angel at work," Beth said.

"It was a miracle for sure," replied Burt.

Dallas looked deep into her eyes. "I believe in miracles, they're all around us if you choose to see them." He pulled her ponytail, arching her neck and he leaned forward to kiss her neck. She pulled away from Dallas.

"We're going to need a miracle not to get shot today. Let's go get this devilment over with," she reached in the saddle bag. She held something up that looked like a big pill. "Now that's what you call a horse pill." She gave each horse one of them. They all laughed and mounted their horse.

~~~~~

They stopped to let the horses get water from the creek. It only took about fifteen minutes to make it to the big Chalet where the casino people lived. In the driveway they left a message from all four horses.

Burt laughed. "I hope they get the message. I wish I could see their reactions." They rode away.

"That white hummer will be real pretty with horse crap all over it. I would love to see that." They all rode away laughing.

~~~~~

They zigzagged back down the mountain trail and were almost at the bottom. Suddenly all the horses became skittish. Burt pulled out his gun and looked around. They spotted several coyotes running through the woods. Burt quickly took aim and shot one. Dallas shot another.

Sierra's horse bolted at the second shot but, she held on tight. She grabbed an arrow and the bow. She took aim, fired and killed a third one. The fourth coyote chased an animal. Sierra thought it was a rabbit but, she continued the chase. The animal dodged the coyote several times. Sierra got closer and realized it was a dog.

The others followed her through the field.

She guided Comet to run right at the coyote, and at the precise moment she lowered her body over the side. She held to the quiver and snatched the dog up just before the coyote pounced on him.

The coyote was startled and paused, before he turned to run away.

Both men fired and hit the coyote twice. He tumbled through the brush and lay there lifeless.

The little beagle dog was rescued at last. He licked Sierra's face between panting.

Dallas raced to her side. "Are you alright," as he circled her.

"Yeah, look at this little guy."

"Where the heck did that come from?"

"I guess he's a stray." She snuggled him up to her neck. He continued to circle her. "I mean you riding like that?"

"Oh, that was nothing," she smiled.

"You could've been killed."

Burt and Beth rode up. Burt gave her a high five. "That was awesome, you've still got it. She was a trick rider as a kid," he smiled and pranced around her.

"What." Dallas hesitated, "You are amazing. I'm just gonna' have to call you Artemis from now on."

"Why, who's that?" She nudged the horse to start walking, holding the little dog.

"Artemis was a Greek goddess that protected the animals. You're just like her, especially with that bow. I couldn't believe what I was seeing," he trotted beside her. "Unbelievable."

"Well, I am from the Wolf Clan, and we are the protectors. So, I guess it is similar to this Artemis."

"Yeah, it sounds like it. I would love to know more about the Cherokee heritage."

"I'm not one to tell you. Maybe we could go to Cherokee one day and do some research."

"I think they have a museum, don't they? I'm sure we could learn a lot there." Dallas suggested.

"We will just have to do that this summer. You would probably love to see the play 'Unto These Hills.'"

"What is that about?" he nudged his horse to get closer to her. "The Trail of Tears."

~~~~~

That night they sat around the fire pit, played with the dog, sang songs, and ate. Dallas and Burt took turns picking the guitar. Sierra moved closer to Dallas and was playing with his hair.

He pulled her onto his lap. "What are you going to name that pup?"

"I don't know. I like the way he moved around the coyotes."

Dallas thought a minute, "How about Sprocket? I had a real smart dog one time and that was his name. I trained him to do tricks."

"That's cool and different. Hey Sprocket, come here," she patted her leg.

He came straight to her and jumped in her lap. He curled up.

"You are definitely Artemis."

Beth and Burt agreed, shaking their heads.

"She is special alright, I couldn't agree more," Burt said as he winked at Sierra.

"Well, this Artemis and Sprocket are exhausted. It's been a long day." She got up and pulled Dallas to his feet. She hugged Burt and Beth. "Thank you for dinner, I hope to see you again soon."

"Yeah, sure. I would like that," Beth replied.

"Good night. It was good to meet you, Beth," Dallas followed Sierra.

"Sunalei," they said.

~~~~~

Dallas sat on the sofa and Sierra laid across his lap while she played with Sprocket, and they listened to music. Dallas started to rub her back, "You scared me out there today."

"Oh, that feels good. I hope I didn't hurt it."

"Did you hear what I said?" He noticed her scar. "What happened to your back?"

She rolled over. "You're full of questions. Which one do you want me to answer?"

"Any of them, all of them."

"I'm sorry I scared you. I didn't have time to explain first." She kissed him lightly. "My back has pins and a plate in it. It was broken in the accident that killed my parents. I was in the back seat, not buckled, laying down. I was thrown a long way, but if I had been buckled, I would have been killed."

"Another miracle."

"I guess, but you don't think about it like that at the time. It took a long time for me to feel that way."

"You were young so, of course. That could be true for anybody."

"Hey, you never told me how many kids you want," not letting him off the hook.

He grinned and tried to avoid her eyes for fear she could see his thoughts. "I told you, it depends."

She held his face so he had to look in her eyes, "Depends on what?"

He started to laugh. "Why did you pull away from me today and not let me kiss your neck?"

"You're changing the subject, Dallas. Why do men always do that?"

He licked his lips, "Just tell me why?"

She watched his tongue. "You know why."

"I want to hear you say it."

She felt her neck and face heat up and fire ran through her body.

"Say it," he pleaded and squeezed her tighter.

"Because…it…makes me want you…" she closed her eyes and leaned into his lips, but she only let the tip of her tongue circle his lips.

He pulled her in and pressed his lips to hers and breathed her in, working slowly down her neck.

"You're right, this is torture. Yet, if I can't kiss you, I think I might die," she whispered. They continued to kiss for a while. She said, "Will you just hold me for a while? I love being in your arms. You make me feel so safe."

"I would love to hold you."

She curled up with him and he played with her hair. She soon fell asleep in the safety of his arms. He softly whispered as he held her, "With you, a dozen. You are so beautiful." He slipped out from underneath her, placed a pillow under her head and covered her with a blanket. He wrote a note and left it on the fridge. Sprocket curled up beside her. He kissed her on the head, "Good night, Artemis."

The next morning, Sprocket licked her face. She muttered, "Stop it, Dallas, that tickles." Sprocket licked her until she woke up. She realized it wasn't Dallas and it was morning.

~~~~~

Dallas and Sierra spent every moment together they possibly could. It was hard to work the ranch, supervise workers, and Dallas' schedule. Sierra reported the beagle to animal control and waited for two weeks, but no one claimed him.

Sierra took Sprocket to Dallas' clinic for shots and a chip. She walked through the door. Dallas stood up from behind the desk to greet her, "Hey, you just made my day," he kissed her. "Come on back, let's check you out," he shut the door.

She handed Sprocket to him, "He's mine now."

He sat the pup on the floor and picked her up. He sat her on the table.

"What are you doing?" she laughed.

Dallas started at her ankles. "Checking you out," he squeezed each leg and moved them in and out. He put his strong hands around her tiny waist, making her arch her back. He slid her closer to him. He put his hand over her heart with the stethoscope and listened to her racing heartbeat. He looked down at Sprocket. "So far, so good." He placed his hands around her head, so his thumbs were in front of her ears. He stood and looked into her eyes. He started to kiss her, stopped, looked at her, started to kiss her, then rubbed her ears. She laughed. "I think you picked a good one, little fella," he said to Sprocket. Sprocket sat and watched them. Dallas looked at Sierra, wrapped his arms around her, and kissed her. He partially laid her on the table and held her. She smiled at him. He started singing, "I'd sure love to lay you down...." Their hearts were beating together like thunder. "Will you go to church with me Sunday?"

She nodded yes, "I'll go anywhere with you." They kissed.

TAKING CHANCES

The next day Travis, Tyler, and Taylor worked on the entry to the ranch. They laid block and stacked stone. The guys were playing music and singing as they worked. Sierra walked down to see their progress. She was surprised by what they were singing as she approached.

She also had a company installing new black fencing along the front and along the driveway.

Dylan and Landyn played music as they painted the bus. She stopped and asked them to go to church on Sunday, but they were reluctant.

~~~~~

Sierra, Burt, and Beth sat down to talk.

"Beth has some leads for us by searching records at the courthouse. These are names of property owners that gave up land for development of the casino and ski slopes."

"That's a lot of people to track down." Sierra looked at the list.

"I'll handle this. You have your hands full." Burt reached for the list.

"I do have my hands full, but I feel so scatter brained sometimes. Ever since I met Dallas my mind stays on him. By the way, Dallas asked me to go to church with him Sunday. Why don't y'all come, too."

They looked at her over the papers, then at each other. "We can do that."

"Dallas said, 'It's important in a meaningful relationship to be equally yoked.' What does that mean?"

"Your beliefs in Christ need to be the same. It's important to have the same Christian beliefs to raise a family successfully." Beth laid down some paper.

"When you have Christ in your relationship, the love you share is like no other. You can conquer the storms of life with faith in Christ," Burt added.

"Maybe that's why so many people get a divorce," Sierra looked over at them.

"Sounds like things are getting serious between you two."

"I guess...if going to church is that important in a serious relationship."

"Absolutely beyond a doubt." Beth smiled at her.

"I just know I'm having a hard time trying to control myself with him. I want him like I've never wanted anyone before. He drives me...crazy," she ran her fingers through her hair. "I think he feels the same way but, I'm not sure."

Burt grinned at her. "That's true love, honey."

She flopped over on the couch. "Ohhh, why does it have to be so complicated?" She hugged a pillow. "He turns my brain and body to mush."

Burt and Beth laughed out loud.

Burt said, "I know you'll make good decisions for yourself. Have you ever heard the scripture "the sins of the flesh can ruin a nation?""

"No, what does that mean?" She sat up still hugging the pillow.

"Let me just say, there are a lot of confused people in the world. God destroyed Sodom and Gomorrah with brimstone and fire. They were two evil cities."

"Aw, Burt don't be so close minded. Everybody has masculine and feminine energy. They just need to learn how to balance it."

"The heck you say, there is nothing feminine about me," he cocked his head and stuck out his chest with his hands on his hips.

She answered with her own sarcasm, "Oh, really."

"Really," he tossed some papers on to the table. "What about when you packed away all Mom and Dad's things so carefully. That was your caring and loving side."

"That was different."

"What about the way you care for all the animals?"

"Beth, I'm going outside before I ring her neck," and he quickly left and shut the door rather loud.

Beth said, "I think you got under his skin a little bit and touched on a nerve. You know men have been taught to hide that sensitive side. They want to be big and tough."

"I know. People need to realize it's okay for men to talk about their feelings or for little boys to play with dolls. It helps them to grow up to be good daddy's or doctors." Sierra moved over to the table.

"We know that, but there are a lot of people out there who will never get that. Now let me finish telling you about Lot and his wife."

Sierra propped her elbow on the table and cupped her chin in her hand, "Okay, tell me."

"When Lot's wife didn't want to leave, she looked back and became a pillar of salt. In today's world, prostitution and abortion would be just two sins of the flesh, but there are many more."

"I could never have an abortion, even if the father didn't want to marry me. I would love that baby no matter what."

"I wish everybody felt that way. I think that's between a woman and God," Beth said.

"You know, when Mary was pregnant with Jesus, Elizabeth was pregnant with John the Baptist.

She was an old woman. When the two came together, Elizabeth's baby leaped in her womb just to hear Mary's voice."

"How could an old woman be pregnant?"

"Because through God, all things are possible," Beth said.

~~~~~

Sunday came, and when they arrived at the church Travis, Taylor, and Tyler were sitting there. Dallas and Sierra sat down by the guys. The guys got up together and went to the front to sing. It was the same song they were singing as they worked, 'Only Jesus.' Dallas came back to sit by her and grinned. He put his arm around her.

"Why didn't you tell me?" she whispered.

He nudged her and grinned sheepishly. "I wanted it to be a surprise," he whispered.

The preacher talked about sins of the flesh and Sodom and Gomorrah. When there was prayer, Dallas either held her tighter or held her hand. The preacher talked about giving your life to Christ. He died on the cross for all sins past, present, and future.

"Jesus has to live through us," he said. When he gave the alter call and older man and a young girl went to the alter.

Sierra noticed Dylan and Landyn sitting in the back and gave them a thumbs up.

~~~~~

On the way home, Sierra rode with Dallas.
He said, "I have a surprise for this evening."
"Oh yeah, you're just full of surprises today."
"Do you trust me?"
"Yeah, until you give me a reason not to."
He picked up her hand and kissed it.

~~~~~

After lunch, Dallas got something out of his car and loaded it on the four-wheeler. "Let's take a ride."

They went on the mountain and ran through creeks. Sierra held to him tight. They went all the way to Devil's Courthouse.

"Alright, moment of truth. I'm going to find out if you really do trust me." He pointed down.

"We're going down there."

"I don't know if I can do this," she stepped backward.

Dallas pulled her hand toward him. "I'll be right beside you. We'll do it together," he strapped the harness tight around her.

"Oh Jesus, Jesus, Jesus," her voice quivered. "I don't like this."

He tried to comfort her. "The scariest part is getting over the ledge." They both climbed over.

"Now, walk with me down and just go slow." They scaled down the rocky wall.

"This is kind of fun. I still don't like to look down." She kept repelling her way down.

"There's a ledge right here, not much further to go." Mist from the waterfall was spraying on them. "Come with me, follow the ledge."

She followed him underneath the waterfall. "This is so cool! I never knew this was here."

It was loud and the roar of the river passed over them. He gave her a hug. "You do trust me."

They climbed down the rocks by the river and then back up through the woods. They walked on fallen trees and crawled under some.

"Hey, look! Here's a dead tree. Let's push it over." Sierra

started pushing, but it would not budge. Dallas started to push with her, and it started to crackle. They pushed even harder, and it started to lean.

"One more big push, come on. We got this!"

They pushed again and it came crashing to the ground. It echoed up the canyon.

"That was awesome. This is way more fun than Cross-Fit." They climbed a steep embankment to get back to the four-wheeler.

"I'm so glad to see that," her leg was shaking.

~~~~~

On the way back down she said, "Stop here a minute. I want to ask you something."

He turned off the engine.

"Do you think that a zip-line could be put in here? It won't even mess up the trails."

He looked around. "I don't see why not, it's a good idea," he patted her leg.

"We can use that old logging road to get people up here. They would enjoy the ride and the view once they're up here. They can hike or ride horses."

Dallas was getting curious about why Sierra wanted to do so much at the ranch. What was her connection to Burt? Why was everything about her such a mystery?

~~~~~

At her cabin, Dallas was quiet.

"What are all these notebooks?" Dallas pulled one off the shelf.

Sierra took it away and slid it back on the shelf. "That's my hopes and dreams, prayers, letters to Mom and Dad, my innermost thoughts and feelings. Hope started me doing that when I went to live with them. I start a new one every year," she replied. "Hey, do you want to watch a movie," she reached for the remote.

"Sure," he said, as he sat down on the sofa.

She sat beside him and scrolled through the movies. "Do you see one you like?"

"No, I want to see a movie about Sierra Wilson. I want to know everything about you," he looked at her.

Sprocket jumped into her lap, and she carried him to the door to let him outside. "Do you want something to drink?" she went to the kitchen. "I need a double..."

Dallas clasped his hands together and squeezed. He suddenly

got up from the sofa and came to the kitchen.

Sierra turned up a shot glass, but he grabbed it out of her hand before she could drink it.

"Please talk to me. Who is Burt to you? What are you hiding from me? What is so bad you can't tell me?" he begged.

She cupped her hands over her tear-filled eyes and face. She sobbed as she paced in the kitchen, "Just stop, stop with all the questions." Her heart felt like it was in her throat. "Just give me a minute," she held her hands up. She wiped away tears.

He leaned against the counter and watched her.

"I want to tell you, but it's really hard. I've never told anyone. Ever." She continued to sob and tried to catch her breath. "I'm afraid it will push you away."

Dallas walked over to her and put his arms around her. He held her and let her cry as he stroked her hair. "You won't push me away."

"Do you promise?"

"I promise."

"Come in here," she took his hand and led him to the bedroom. They laid across the bed and held each other.

"You're shaking," he covered her with a throw.

"I don't know where to begin, but you have to swear to keep my secret."

"I told you, you can trust me. I swear."

She took a deep breath. "Burt is my mom's brother. He faked my death after the accident that killed my parents."

Dallas' eyes widened.

"But it wasn't an accident, so I had to change my name. I lived with James and Hope in Dallas, NC. I went."

He interrupted, "Wait, what's your name?"

"I was born Abigail Diana Turner."

He sat forward on the bed.

"See, this is going to push you away. I know it."

"No, it's not. Tell me."

"My mom was Diana Gayle, and my dad was Tom," she pointed to their picture.

"I am so sorry. Are you really a veterinarian?"

"Yes, I went to school in Georgia and lived there for a while." She blew her nose. "My mom was Cherokee. She rode trick horses and Roman riding. They taught me. My dad was Spanish-

American and a bullfighter. Most of his people are in Spain. I went to Spain after college and my cousins taught me how to bullfight."

Dallas got the picture, "You look like you mom. That's why in church some people thought they were seeing a ghost."

She nodded her head yes. "I had hoped you didn't hear that," she sniffled.

He sat down on the bed. "What do you mean that it was no accident?"

"Someone tried to kill all of us."

Dallas' eyes widened in surprise, "God bless you, poor thing." He pulled her head toward him and kissed her forehead. "No wonder you didn't want to tell me, this is horrible."

"Burt has some evidence, but no one has ever been able to solve it."

He put his arms around her.

"No one can know the truth right now. I have to remain Sierra. You know the big farmhouse you liked on the other side of the mountain?"

He nodded yes and listened intensely.

"That's where I lived with my parents," she started to sob again.

Dallas wiped away her tears.

"I wasn't prepared to tell my story. I wasn't prepared for you. Do you understand?" She laid her hand on his and squeezed.

"I do, and don't worry. I will do anything to protect you," he lifted her chin. "Do you understand?"

She nodded yes and hugged him.

He kissed her lips and held her until she stopped crying. "You know Diana is another name for Artemis?"

She chuckled. "I want to know more about you. I know your mom named you Dallas because you were born in Dallas, Texas. You have a big family, but you don't talk about them."

"Well, I have an older brother. Travis, Taylor, and Tyler are his kids."

"What's his name?"

"Dennis. There are four girls, I'm the youngest. I have six nieces and nephews. Everybody is scattered."

"How did you get to NC?"

He did a driving motion with his hands. "Got in the car and drove."

She playfully pinched him. "You know what I mean. Why did you pick NC?"

"Jesse and Jenna had a friend named Cindi. Well, Cindi came to Austin for a veterinarian symposium, and I met her. She carried on about NC and the Smokey Mountains until I had to come and see it for myself. I fell in love with this place. The land and the people, so I stayed. 'Land of the waterfalls' was what Cindi called it."

"When was that symposium, because I went to Austin to one."

"Four years ago, I think."

"And that's when a big hurricane hit, I thought I would never get back home. I was stuck in the airport for days."

"Don't tell me we were at the same one."

They said together, "We were at the same one."

"What a small world we live in."

"You got that right."

They just sat there thinking about it.

Sierra finally gathered her thoughts, "So, what about your mom and dad?"

"We lost Dad a long time ago, and Mom a few years ago. I think she grieved herself to death, she loved him so much. She was different after Dad passed away."

"Do you keep in touch with your family?"

"Some of them. We…haven't been the same since Mom passed. That's when us boys came here, to get away from all the bickering. I haven't spoken to my brother in four years."

"I can't imagine that."

"It's a long story. I promise I'll tell you someday." He kissed her and held her tight. "Do you feel better getting that off your chest?"

"Yeah, I do. It's like a huge burden has been lifted off me."

"Good. What did you think of the sermon today?"

"That was good, I liked the preacher and…the singing. We talked about Sodom and Gomorrah yesterday. That's weird that he preached about it today."

"Sometimes it feels like the message is just for you."

"That was good two people got saved today."

Dallas said, "Always good when that happens. I assume you have been saved."

She nodded yes. "And you?"

He shook his head. "You know what, it's getting late."

Sierra looked at the clock, "It's 11:11. I didn't realize how late it was." They got up from the bed and made their way to the door. "I could sit and talk to you forever," she added.

"We can definitely get into some deep subjects," he opened the door. "Thank you for trusting me and taking a chance," he took both his hands and held hers. He kissed them before he walked away.

FEELING FREE

That night, Sierra dreamed of three white horses running on the beach. She rode the middle horse and held her arms out. She felt free.

~~~~~

Dallas went to work, but the day was not a typical day. A client brought in a stray. It was one of the men from the casino, Alan Dabadee. Conversation started as a typical client, and he seemed nice enough. Then the conversation turned personal.

"I saw you at the New Year's party. You looked like you were having a good time with that young lady."

He turned away from him. "She's special, that's for sure."

"Where did you learn to dance like that?"

"College, I thought it might come in handy someday."

"Turned out you were right," he crossed his arms. "Who's the girl? I've never seen her before?"

Dallas turned to look him square in the eye, "She just moved here. That was actually our first date."

"She certainly was a lovely girl."

"Yes, she is, thank you," he took the leash and handed it to him. "Thanks for bringing Chester in, he's ready to go."

Dallas watched him as he left and wondered, 'Now why do you care about Sierra?'

Mr. Dabadee stopped at the concrete plant.

~~~~~

Burt was busy doing his own investigation. He noticed some

Chinese names on some of the deeds. One particular property had burned to the ground, that also caught his interest. He tracked down the former owner.

The man said, "It was arson, so I got no insurance money. I had to sell, I still have the paperwork. The Chinese bought it. It had been in my family for five generations. I sure hope you can catch whoever is responsible."

Most of the casino's land had once belonged to old man Johnson, who passed away. The casino got it through an auction. Mr. Johnson had no relatives. He dug further into Mr. Johnson's death. It was deemed that he had died of a heart attack. There were defensive bruises on his body. At that time, it was thought to be normal for his age and being on blood thinner. Burt looked up from the paperwork. "I'll be damned. They beat him into a heart attack."

~~~~~

Johnny and Dylan took the bus to town and left it for new graphics to be put on.

Landyn stayed behind to do chores. He mucked the stalls.

Sierra walked in and found Landyn smoking a joint. He quickly threw it in the manure and stomped it.

"I know what that smell is, you're not fooling me." She pointed her finger at his nose. "This is not going to fly. All I have to do is make a phone call and you'll go to jail."

'Yes, ma'am."

"There are no more warnings, do you get it?"

"Yes, ma'am." He shot up his middle finger at her when she turned around.

She checked the horses' hooves. "You're going to have to do a better job keeping the muck out of their hooves," she pulled muck out with her hand and threw it on the ground. "This is unacceptable."

Landyn made faces behind her.

"Get every one of these done after you muck the stalls."

"I will," he scornfully replied as he continued his task.

Sprocket was by her side and growled at Landyn. He kicked toward the dog and Sprocket barked.

She quickly turned and got about an inch from his nose. "Don't ever kick my dog or mistreat an animal here!"

He stood there and looked down while he held the pitchfork.

"I'll be on you like stink on crap!"

Johnny and Dylan turned the corner in time to hear that remark.

"What's going on?" Johnny asked.

She looked at Landyn. "Nothing, right Landyn?"

He indicated, "Just a misunderstanding. That's all."

She turned to Johnny and whispered, "I hope I nipped it in the bud," and she walked away.

Johnny gave Landyn and evil eye. "She can do it, too."

Sierra turned Bam-Bam out to the arena and took a muleta.

Dylan watched her from the loft above and overlooking the arena. "Landyn, come up here. You gotta' see this."

Landyn scurried up to the loft.

"She's done this before."

"Who is she, anyway?"

"I don't know, but you better not make her mad. There's no telling what she's capable of doing."

"Ah, I'm not scared of her. She's a girl."

"Landyn, I'm telling you. You better watch yourself."

Bam-Bam and Sierra seemed to be having a good time. Then Sierra tripped in the thick dirt. She landed face down and when she rolled over, Bam-Bam was headed straight for her. She braced for impact. Bam-Bam stopped right over the top of her and began to lick her face. Diesel came out and barked at Bam-Bam. Dylan and Landyn came running, expecting her to be hurt. She laid in the dirt, laughing. Dylan helped her to her feet.

"Thanks, I thought I was a goner," she said, still laughing.

"Me too, are you scared of anything?"

"Well, I don't like heights."

"Is that all?"

She studied a minute. "I'm mostly scared of not knowing what comes next," she limped toward the barn. "If I didn't have Jesus Christ in my heart, I would probably do things a lot different. I know if something happens to me, I'm going to Heaven."

"How do you know for sure?"

"Once you open up your heart to Him and accept Him as your Savior, your life is changed forever. You'll know it when it happens. Are you guys not saved?"

"No, we never went to church much. Mama tried."

"Well, you can get saved anywhere."

There was silence. "A church I went to when I was a kid had a picture on the wall. Jesus was knocking on the door, but there was no doorknob. I asked my mother why and she said, 'The only way Jesus can get in is you open the door when He knocks.' It's the only way to get to Heaven. Your name will be in the Lamb's Book of Life when you get to the Pearly Gate."

The guys listened intensely. They sat down on some bales of hay.

"I'm glad y'all went to church Sunday. I know there's a Bible in the cabin. I can get another one so each of you have one."

"It's hard to understand all that stuff."

"That's why you need to go to church, it helps. Read John 3:16 and remember it. 'For God so loved the world He gave His only son, that whoever believed in Him would not perish but have everlasting life."

"How can you remember that?"

"It's about the most important verse in the Bible. Any time you guys want to talk, just find me.

Okay?" She stood up.

Dylan said, "I'm not sure I can believe in something I can't see."

She sat back down.

"That's what faith is. Jesus is all around, you just have to choose to see it. I'll give you an example."

"I know a man named Curtis. Him and his wife lived in Florida. They moved to Georgia. Curtis was told by an angel to go on this mountain. Well, it was a long way away. Curtis went to another mountain. When he got there, some men were cutting trees. So, Curtis left, and he went to the mountain he was supposed to. This was a big man and he got scared. He saw an angel that was colors he had never seen before. This angel told him to get a book on healing."

"Now, they had just moved to Georgia and didn't know anybody. They went to church and a man approached him. This man said, 'I believe you're Curtis and you have a book for me.' Sierra laughed, "Now how do you think that's possible?"

The guys were completely intrigued by her and sat there.

"Tell us another one," Landyn said.

"That's cool," Dylan replied.

"Do you ever wonder why things happen the way they do?"

"Yeah, strange things."

"One day I needed to get up early and go from NC to Georgia. I was so tired I couldn't get up when the alarm went off. On the way down I-85, there was a terrible accident. A lot of people got killed and multiple vehicles burned up. If I had left when I was supposed to, I would have been right there at the time of the accident."

"Wow."

Sierra got up, "Y'all finish your chores, get those hooves cleaned, the day is almost gone. I'll give you something to think about. Ask yourself, 'What are my chances without God in my life?'"

~~~~~

Sierra walked down to the entry of the ranch. The guys were stacking stone. They were playing music.

"This looks great guys. I'm loving it already. I know how I want the gate, but I can't get it made till you're done with this part."

Travis started swinging her around and Tyler and Taylor joined in. They were all laughing and dancing.

Dallas pulled in and sat watching them.

Travis said, "Daddy's home, we're in trouble now!" He went running to Dallas' truck and said,

"Welcome home honey, how 'bout a kiss." He stuck his head in the window and puckered his lips.

Dallas pulled his head back and said, "I'll beat your ass, Travis."

Sierra stopped dancing and looked at him. Her heart turned a flip. She didn't know what to think. She got in the truck and said, "Hey, can I bum a ride. These guys are crazy."

"Well, I don't want to sound judgmental, but you looked like you were having a good time," he raised his eyebrows.

She defended herself, "I just got there, to check on the progress. They did a lot today. Do you like it?"

"Yeah." He drove up to the cabin.

She tried to redirect the conversation. "How was your day?"

"Busy…interesting." They got out of the truck.

Sierra walked around and cupped her hands around his face and kissed him.

"I needed that," he wrapped his arms around her waist.

"I needed my eye candy today," she kissed him again.

"I've thought about you a lot today."

She leaned toward him. "You did?" She took his hand and walked backward, pulling him toward her. "What were you thinking?"

He followed her.

~~~~~

Inside the cabin, she leaned on the wall and slipped off her boots.

He shut the door and hung up their coats. He turned to her and put his hands on the wall. She was between his hands. She started to breathe harder, and her heart raced. He turned his head slightly and leaned closer. She could smell his cologne, she put her arms around his waist. His head rubbed against hers as his lips fell on her shoulder. He slowly kissed up the side of her neck.

Chill bumps spread over her body. He slipped one hand under her hair at her neck and moved her hair behind her shoulder. The other arm he placed in the small of her back. He lifted her but kept her against the wall. She wrapped her legs around him and cupped his face in her hands. Their open lips pressed together, as did their bodies. It was hard to breathe. He turned and carried her to the kitchen counter and sat her down on the counter.

Both were shaking as they looked in each other's eyes. They held each other, closed their eyes and rested their heads on each other's shoulders.

"Now I know what you were thinking today."

"Mmmm-huh."

She ran her fingers through his hair, "Would you like some dinner to go with that dessert?"

He laughed, "Yes I would."

They shared each other's days' events while they ate and then moved to the sofa.

"What went through your mind today when you saw me with the guys? I've never seen that side of you before," she put her leg over his.

He leaned toward her and put his arm around her. "That makes two of us. I guess I've never had a girl I cared enough about to feel jealous when I saw her with another man. I know those guys would never. They know better than to do that to me."

She assured him, "We were just goofing off."

"But I didn't like it." He took her hand, "I guess what I'm trying to say is, I want you...all of you...to myself."

She kissed him. "I feel the same way, but I'm glad you told me. I would never be unfaithful to you. Ever."

He rubbed her leg. "You know I see the way people look at you."

"But I can't help the way I look, and I can't control other people. I think women hate me. I think men are intimidated around me, or just want to use me. That's why I love animals, I can be myself. They don't care what I look like," she looked down.

He pulled her chin up to look at her, "Do you think I just want to use you?"

She hesitated, "I hope not." Her heart ached. "I think the pain in my heart would be unbearable if you did that to me." Her eyes began to well up with tears at the thought of it.

He saw the pain in her eyes. "I could never do that to you, ever." He wiped away a tear and kissed her. "So, if I asked you not to see anyone else, can I trust you?" he squeezed her leg.

"One hundred percent, but that road goes both ways. None of this having your cake and eating it, too." Their fingers laced together. "So, can I trust you to be faithful to me?"

"Absolutely."

They hugged and kissed.

LOVE ENDURES

Days passed by and Sierra did not hear from Dallas. She tried to call and text, but she heard nothing from him. She wanted to go see him at the clinic but was afraid to. It was all she could think about. She thought, 'Did I make him mad at me, but why. I don't understand, things were going so great. Maybe I scared him away. Maybe it was too good to be true.' No matter how she tried to reason it out in her head it made no sense. She curled up on her bed and cried and she cried for days. It felt like her heart had been stabbed with a dagger.

Before going to bed Sierra prayed for guidance and clarity.

The next morning, she heard Sprocket jump down off the bed and shake himself.

Before she opened her eyes, she saw angels come to her, and lift her from her bed. She was not afraid, all she felt was peace and love. Her body became a light and up ahead was another light. She was surrounded by blue, and it sparkled. She floated toward the light that was inside strands of different colors, and the colors swirled around the light. When she reached the light, and it was revealed to her that it was Dallas. They immediately embraced each other.

Suddenly she was back in her bed and opened her eyes. She sat up and became overwhelmed with tears. 'What had just happened.' She thought, 'Surely that was God that answered my prayer.' Sierra found the strength to rise from her bed and she felt so much joy in her heart at what she had experienced. She felt as if everything was going to be alright. There was such a magnetic pull to Dallas. She could not resist the love she felt for him.

~~~~~

Sierra watched Burt and Beth. She could tell their relationship was special. Sierra approached Beth. "Hey, can I ask you something?"

"Sure," she put down a hose from watering the horses. "Is everything okay. We wondered if you and Dallas had an argument."

"No argument, I guess he needed some time to sort a few things out. I'm just giving him his space."

"Sometimes that's the only thing you can do."

"I suppose. Well, you know Valentine's Day is in a couple of days and I've never had anyone special when it rolled around. I want to get Dallas something special, but I don't know where to start."

"I can always find something at the Christian Bookstore. They have way more than books. Why don't you start there? Maybe something will jump out at you."

"Okay, thanks."

~~~~~

At the bookstore, Sierra was amazed at the things to choose from. She looked through the music and decided on a CD. Her eyes fell on some jewelry, it seemed to jump at her.

Sierra pointed to a bracelet. "Can I see this one?"

"This one is nice to put an engraving on."

"Can you do that here?"

"We sure can," she shook her head yes.

"Okay, I'll take this one."

"What would you like engraved on it?" She thought for a minute and smiled.

When she left, she felt excited and pleased with her find. "For once I'm actually looking forward to Valentine's Day." She decided to call him. They began to talk, and it felt as though they had never been apart.

~~~~~

Valentine's Day couldn't come soon enough. She was nervous and excited. She had prepared dinner, lit candles throughout the cabin, and played soft music. Her hair was partially pulled back and she wore a sexy red dress.

Sprocket followed her around smelling the candles. She looked out the door to see Burt and Beth riding Prince and Duchess. The sun was setting, and it was a perfect sailor's delight. It was chilly, so she turned on the gas logs and waited for Dallas.

He approached the door, dressed in church clothes and she opened the door. He handed her a dozen long stem red roses. "Happy Valentine's Day, Sweetheart."

"Thank you," she accepted the flowers in one hand and pulled him to her with the other. "Happy Valentine's Day to you. You look and smell delicious." They kissed.

"You look amazing, as always," he twirled her around. He held one hand behind his back.

She laid the flowers on the counter. He never let go of her hand.

She came back to him and wrapped her arms around his waist. She felt the box he was holding.

"What's that?" she smiled.

He kept the box out of her reach.

She tried to get it. "Don't tease me."

He switched it to the other hand. "It's just a box; it's something for later. Dinner smells awesome."

"Oh, I need to get it out of the oven. I hope I didn't burn it," she said as she grabbed a mitt and reached in the oven, "it's eggplant parmesan."

He laid the flowered box down by the sofa. Then he leaned against the wall. "I love eggplant parm," he folded his arms over his chest and watched her move about the kitchen.

She asked, "Are you hungry?"

"I'm always ready for your good cooking."

"Well let's eat then," she sliced the dish and took each a plate to the candlelit table.

They held hands and Dallas said the blessing. "Lord, thank you for this meal and the hands that prepared it. Bless this food to the nourishment of our bodies, and our bodies to thy service. Amen."

"This looks wonderful," he took a bite. "Oh my gosh, that's so good. Hot, but good. This is one of my faves."

"Me, too. I'm glad you like it. I made cheesecake for dessert," she smiled at him.

"For real," he smiled. "Are you trying to fatten me up?"

"No, just spoil you a little."

"Well, you are. I don't cook like this just for me. It's no fun cooking for yourself."

"I know what 'cha mean," she took another bite. "Burt and Beth are coming over for dessert. later. They rode up to Paradise Point for the sunset."

"It was a pretty day for a ride, it's gonna be cold tomorrow though."

"Spring can't get here soon enough."

They cleared the table and stood by the fire.

She reached for her gift to him and he opened it and smiled. "I love it." He looked inside, "Do everything in love, I'll walk through fire for you. Sierra." He placed it on his wrist, "That's deep, thank you."

They wrapped their arms around each other and kissed. They began to dance around the cabin. Her hair glistened with the flicker of the fire, and he played with her hair. Then he turned her around and held her close. She laid her head on his shoulder. He kissed her neck and then turned her face to his and kissed her lips.

She turned to face him, and they slowly danced over to the gift box he had for her. He said, "Don't get excited, this is something for later," he handed her the box.

She lifted out a silky white night gown with spaghetti straps and lace. There was a slit up the thigh. "It's beautiful," she held it against her.

"It will be beautiful on you someday, when the time is right. For now, I'm just going to leave it to my imagination. I can dream about taking if off of you."

"Thank you," she cupped his face with her hands and kissed him.

They were still dancing when Burt and Beth arrived. Burt held out Beth's hand to show off the ring he gave her.

"It's about time, Burt!" Sierra hugged both of them. "Congratulations."

Beth said, "It only took him fifteen years. I thought I was going to have to ask him."

"What can I say, I'm a man with a slow hand."

Dallas started singing and Burt joined him as the couples danced around the room. Sprocket was curled up by the fireplace but livened up when Sierra brought out the cheesecake. She cut two big slices, one for each couple. Sierra gave Dallas a big bite with a cherry on top.

"Mmm," he savored the bite.

~~~~~

Sierra and Dallas' love for each other continued to grow every day. One night they went to dinner and the waitress said, "A blind man could see that you two are in love."

~~~~~

March brought an early spring that year, and with it came hard work on the ranch. Some trees were being cut to make way for the zip-line. They used the track hoe and an old tractor. One day the old tractor puttered out. It was done. Sierra went to town, and when she came back home, she had two new tractors.

Dylan said, "Tractors are green, why did you get these?"

"Because we needed them, and tractors are red. Now the work can get done twice as fast, one for each of you."

Dylan and Landyn climbed on the tractors and started checking them out.

Sierra shook her head. "Boys and their toys, boys and their toys." They raced down the driveway. She yelled after them, "Break my tractor and I'll break your heads."

~~~~~

Dallas came by to see her after work. He couldn't find anybody, but he heard a chain saw running across the pasture. He got on the four-wheeler and went in that direction. Just over the hill, he stopped. Sierra had the chain saw cutting trees into firewood. She had on jeans, work boots, a hard hat, and a flannel shirt tied around her waist. He could see her muscular arms as she worked the saw. He shook his head and thought, 'She is one of a kind.'

She was unaware he was watching her. He headed toward her. She looked up and smiled to acknowledge his presence. "Did you come to rescue me?" She rested the saw on her shoulder and walked toward him.

"I guess I did, if you need rescuing. I sure didn't come to make you mad. You might chop me up in little pieces," he was serious.

"I might just do that," she put the saw on the back of the wheeler and climbed on behind him.

"Go that way," she said, pointing.

Burt and Johnny were using the track hoe to get some big stones out of the river.

"We're building up this low spot, so it doesn't flood," she told

Dallas. She waved at Burt and motioned she was going back. Burt acknowledged her.

Instead of going to the ranch, Dallas turned the wheeler to go up to Paradise Point. The sun had started to set. They got off the wheeler once they reached the peak. Dallas looked out over the mountains and then looked at her. "I'm trying to decide."

She looked puzzled, "Decide on what?"

"Stand over here," he pointed and stepped back a few steps. "That's it, now I can see forever." He took her picture. She posed, puckering her lips and leaned forward with her hand on her knee. He took another picture.

"I think Burt and Beth decided to get married up here."

"There's not a prettier place, that's for sure."

"You know one of our legends is about the bald spots on the top of the mountains."

"Well tell it to me," he pulled her close and wrapped his arms around her.

"The young horses would be separated from their mothers and brought up here, to graze on the spring grass and wean them. Later in the summer they would return to the valley below to join the herd. One year no one returned for the ponies, and they called out, but still no one came. Some say that you can still hear them, screaming."

"Why didn't they come back for them?"

"That was the year of the Trail of Tears."

~~~~~

The next day was Saturday, and the guys were well underway building a shed to store rafts and gear. Tyler was home with the flu. Dallas came over early. Sierra had on a tool belt and her hard hat. She was up on the roof laying shingles and swinging a hammer. Dallas started up the ladder.

She said, "Bring some shingles as you come, don't waste a trip."

"Yes, ma'am," he slung a pack on his shoulder. He climbed up, walked over to her, and put the pack down. He looked at her, took her hat and belt, reached for the hammer, "I got this."

Travis and Taylor never acknowledged Dallas out loud.

Sierra watched Dallas work. She thought, 'He's so sexy.' She got up to move some shingles.

He pointed the hammer at her, "Sit down or I'll carry you off this roof." She sat down at his command. Travis and Taylor stopped and looked at him. Dallas pointed the hammer at them, "Don't say a word."

Travis said, "You can't see me."

They finished the building that day.

~~~~~

Sierra collapsed on the sofa. "Thank you for helping, they need to start platforms for zip lining next week."

Dallas sat in the floor and pulled her boots off. He started to rub her feet. "Do you ever take a minute for yourself?"

"Not too often," she said, shaking her head. "The list is never ending."

"Enough is enough," he got up. He went to the tub and drew her some bath water and filled it full of suds. He lit some candles and put on soft music.

He came back to her, pulled her up from the sofa, and carried her to the bathroom. "Now get in," he commanded.

He called for take-out and delivery. When he went to the bathroom, he took a pitcher. He pulled the braids out of her hair, poured water over her and washed her hair.

"You don't have to be tough all the time," he said softly. "You don't have to fight your battles alone."

SUBMISSION

After church on the way to Dallas' house he said, "I'm fixing you some lunch and you're going to relax," he looked at her and waited for the objection.

She just looked out the window and didn't argue with him. She knew he meant it.

"I want to treat you like a queen, and if you don't let me, I'm going to lock you in my tower," he grinned and kissed her hand.

She sarcastically replied, "I'll submit to you only because you're a Godly man," she squeezed his hand.

It was a rainy day, and the March winds were blowing. Rain began to pour down.

"It's a good thing we're here, I can't see a gosh darn thing." It was a huge house, and the barn was down a long driveway.

"Do you have an umbrella," she asked.

He looked in the car. "I think I left it at church."

"We can make a run for it."

They didn't have far to go but got absolutely drenched. "I don't think an umbrella would have helped, it's a monsoon."

They laughed going into the house.

~~~~~

"Brrr. It's a good day to watch a movie," she shivered.

"Let's get on some dry clothes, lunch will be ready in no time." He rummaged through his clothes and handed her a muscle shirt, sweatshirt, sweatpants, and socks. "This will be comfy." He got the same for himself.

She wandered into the spacious kitchen.

"They're a little big," he looked at her.

"It's okay, it feels good. Can I turn on the fire logs?" she looked in the living room at a stone fireplace.

"Yeah, it's right on the side," he pointed and went back to the food.

"This is beautiful. How many bedrooms does it have?" she looked around.

"Four, the boys lived here when we first came, or I wouldn't have such a big house. They still keep their horses here, though."

She looked at his family pictures. "How old were you in this picture?" She held it up.

"I think I was twenty."

"Do you need some help?" she peeped around the corner.

He pointed his finger at her.

"Just asking." She held up a hand.

They sat down to eat, and a big lightning bolt struck and thunder clapped at the same time.

They both shuddered, the power went out.

"So much for watching a movie."

"A tree probably fell on a power line," he suggested.

"I kinda like big storms. Can't you just feel the power of God?" she shivered.

"That's one way to look at it, I guess."

"This is good soup and cornbread. I'm impressed."

"Thanks. I don't mind cooking if I have someone to share it with. Eat all you want, okay?"

"You have a pretty place. I like the creek out there."

"It's raging right now."

"That's the big thing we have to deal with in the mountains. The flooding, mudslides and down trees."

"I guess every place has its problems."

"They sure do, but I love it in these mountains."

"If you're done, I'll show you around. We'll clean up later." He stood up and reached for her hand.

"Are you gonna show me your tower?"

"No, only if you're bad. I'll take you to the dungeon, though." They went down some steps.

~~~~~

He opened some curtains and turned on a lantern. "I've got a flashlight somewhere that should have batteries in it." He looked on a shelf, "Here we go, we can get some tunes going."

She could see gym equipment everywhere. On one end was a big screen TV, stereo, and pool table. She began to look through his CD's. I've never heard of a lot of these people.

"They're oldies, but goodies. I grew up listening to this stuff. My brother played it all the time. What do you like?"

She saw a big punching bag and walked over to it. "I like everything except rap." He put on some music and walked toward her.

She kept the bag between them, and they circled it. He pushed it toward her. She pushed it back. He kicked it. She kicked it back. Each time was a little harder.

"Okay, I can see you've had some training."

"James taught me, him and Burt were Seals," she punched the bag.

"I didn't know that."

"Well, now you know. Consider it a warning," she looked over her shoulder.

"Oooh, I like confidence. I consider it a challenge." She punched and kicked.

They played around a while and she said, "We better stop while we're ahead."

"You are probably right, somebody might get hurt."

They rested on a mat. Then they got a second wind and started to wrestle. This time, when he pinned her, she broke free.

She pinned him, face down. "Who's submitting to whom?"

He laughed, "Okay, I'll submit to you, only because you're a Godly woman." He wrenched in pain. "And because you're breaking my arm."

She let go. She laid beside him looking up, laughing.

He rolled to his side and propped on his elbow. "Is there anything you can't do?"

She thought a few seconds. "Sure, I just haven't found it yet." She giggled.

"At least I know you can handle yourself if you ever needed to."

"James and Burt made sure of that."

"Can you hear that? That's a big rig, I bet it's the power company."

They both got up and looked out a window. A tree had fallen on the power line just across from his house on the main road.

"Good thing we planned to stay in, that's going to take a while." He turned to face her. He put his arms around her.

She put her arms around him, and they kissed.

"At least the rain stopped. Hey, you can show me your horses."

"Okay, come on." He pulled on some rubber boots.

She pulled off her socks, "I'll just go bare footed."

"Not to the barn, put these on," he handed her a pair of boots that were way too big.

~~~~~

"I can't walk too good in these," she dragged her feet on the way to the barn. At the barn they fed and watered the horses. The sky let loose again. They started to run back to the house while holding hands. Her boots slid in a big mud puddle, and she pulled him down with her. They lay there laughing, getting soaked again and covered in mud. She picked up some mud and threw it at him. He picked up a handful of mud and rubbed on her. They were still laughing when they got up. They stood in the rain kissing. "Just give me a shampoo bottle," she pleaded. A loud clap of thunder and a bolt of lightning made them get it in gear to the house.

~~~~~

They were still laughing when they reached the bathroom. He reached and got her a towel and turned on the shower. He couldn't help but to notice how beautiful she was with mud all over her. He moved a strand of wet muddy hair from her face. She bit her lip. Before he realized what, he was doing, he pulled her muddy sweatshirt over her head and just stood there looking at her raw beauty. Their hearts rumbled like the thunder.

"I'm…going to another bathroom…okay?"

She shook her head yes.

When she got out of the shower, she wrapped the towel around her and looked for some more clothes. She found a Big Dog Motorcycle t-shirt and slipped it over her wet hair.

Dallas came in with only jeans on. He handed her a pair. "I think you can wear these. One of the boys left them here."

"Thanks," she slipped them on. "Do you have a hair dryer?" She was still looking at his pecs and abs going into a V at the top of his jeans. He took the wet towel and when he turned around, she could see his back was chiseled as well.

He turned to look at her, "No, I don't. Sorry," he moved her wet hair.

She felt fire run through her veins. "I'll just sit by the fire for a while."

"If you want to bring some of your things to have a spare here, you can. I don't mind." He picked up the muddy clothes and walked to the bathroom.

She followed him and laid her hand on his shoulder.

He dropped the clothes and turned to face her.

She pushed him against the counter and began to run her fingers across his chest.

He watched her as if she were an artist drawing on a canvas or molding him from clay. He felt helpless.

She traced his muscles with her fingers and glided her hands over his body. She traced his back muscles as she looked in the mirror behind him.

Chill bumps covered his body, and he was paralyzed by her touch.

She moved to his face with both hands and lightly traced his lips with her thumb. She closed her eyes, taking it all in. She kissed him as if to breathe life into her masterpiece.

He reached and pulled her to him against his naked skin and they held each other. They both wanted so much more.

She laced her fingers with his in both hands and raised their arms overhead. She said, "Kiss me." She squeezed his hands and then let go. She glided her fingers down his arms and sides and down the V on his abdomen.

It felt like electricity running through his body and he felt dizzy. "What just happened?"

"Are you okay?"

"No, what did you just do to me?" he gasped for air as he shivered.

She smiled at him and led him to the fire. "I just moved some energy around." She got him a shirt and sat down with him by the fire. "At least the power is back on."

"Yeah," Dallas sat there a while wondering what just happened. After he regained his composure he asked her, "Do you want to watch a movie?"

"Sure, but no chic flicks though. I like action," she said. "You find us one, I'll fix some popcorn," she handed him the remote and

went to the kitchen.
He was quiet throughout most of the movie and just smiled.
The movie had a motorcycle in it.
"Isn't Big Dog a motorcycle?"
"It is."
"Do you have one, do you know how to ride?"
He helped her to her feet and led her to the garage. "That's why I couldn't get the car in." There sat a Big Dog motorcycle. It was black and had a dream catcher painted on the tank.
"That's pretty. I've never rode one."
"You're kidding. Oh my gosh, we'll have a blast on this thing when it gets a little warmer."
"There's something I don't know how to do, drive one."
"Well, I'll have to teach you," he led her back in the house to the sofa.
She thought, 'My birthday is coming up. I'm going to buy me some black leather riding gear.
He won't be expecting that.'
She placed her hand on his thigh. "I want to thank you for a wonderful day…and for not pressuring me to have sex. I know you want to."
He looked at her. "I do, but I don't want another relationship based solely on sex," he played with her hair. "I want more…so much more. I'm happy just being in the same room with you. Today was a fun day." He kissed her.
"I know what we have is special. I don't want to make things complicated. I know that there's a lot of components to a serious relationship. I'm ready for that, I want that…with you." She looked into his eyes.
"I do, too. Communication is huge."
"Faith."
"Common interests and goals."
"Trust."
"Respect."
"Supporting each other."
"Having fun, laughing, playing in mud." They laughed.
"So, we're both…"
They said together, "…on the same page." They kissed and hugged.

TIME MARCHES ON

Sierra constantly had more to do than she could get done. She knew if Dallas found out half the things she did, he would put a stop to it. She decided to hire more help.

This time, she hired females to have some balance on the ranch and some female companionship. She also knew that it could bring on a whole new set of problems. She was willing to take that chance.

The zip-line was almost ready, and the rafts had arrived for rafting. Sierra wanted more horses for trail riding. She was looking online and found an auction that was coming up on Chincoteague Island in July. They were wild horses.

Sierra asked Burt, "What do you think about getting some of these horses?" She showed him the computer.

"You could probably get a good deal, but I've never done an auction before. Then the horses would have to be trained. That would be a job for the next year," he folded his arms over his chest.

"Do you think it would be worth it?"

"Maybe, if you can get the right horses."

"I'll ask Dallas what he thinks. You never told me what you think about the new gate and fence."

"It looks great, everything does. Now, slow down. What are your plans for your birthday?"

"Dallas has made plans. He said I just have to show up," she smiled.

Burt smiled, "He's been good for you." He kissed her head. "I like him a lot. Your parents would've liked him, too."

She smiled at him as he left. "Sgi (Thanks)."

~~~~~

Sierra's birthday arrived and she was nervous not knowing what to expect. When Dallas came to pick her up, she didn't notice the ranch was deserted. He gave her flowers.

She got in the car, and he pulled out a cloth.

"This is a surprise and I'm putting a blindfold on you. No peeking."

"Such a mystery man."

He kissed her passionately. "You're gonna love this."

"I loved that kiss," she held out her hand to find his, and he took it.

~~~~~

He drove her to his house and once inside, he removed the blindfold. Everyone from the ranch and others, plus his nephews were there. They yelled, "Surprise!"

Sierra was overrun with emotion as well as everyone there. Immediately she recognized Jayda, Kate, Pam, Amya and Bobbie. She wiped away a tear, "I don't know how ya'll pulled this off."

Beth said, "It took a lot of work, all of us."

Burt added, "Beth and Hope were the masterminds behind it."

Sierra said, "I can't believe ya'll kept this a secret."

Jayda hugged her, "We couldn't believe the secret you've been keeping all these years."

~~~~~

Courtney and Haylee were hanging out with Dylan, Landyn, Tyler, Taylor, and Travis shooting pool. Sierra and the girls sat talking and catching up. Dallas kept a watchful eye on her. He seemed happy to see her having a good time. They all were.

Dallas joined in a game of pool, but still kept his eye on Sierra. Dallas missed a shot.

Travis said, "You can't make the shot if you're looking at her the whole time."

Sierra tilted her head and looked his way.

The next time it was Dallas' turn, Travis put his face down close to the table and pointed to the hole. "Right here, right here, come on."

Dallas made the ball hit Travis right in the eye.

He held his hand to his eye, "What'd you do that for?"

"Well, I was aiming for your big mouth. Sorry," he laid the pool stick down.

Sierra noticed Dallas leaving the room and she went to the kitchen to look for him.

"What are you doing?" She walked up behind him and wrapped her arms around him.

"Nothing are you okay?" he turned around.

"Never been better. This is the best birthday ever. Thank you."

"We wanted you to know this is a wonderful day and we all celebrate you." He kissed her.

They heard Burt, James, and Johnny in the garage carrying on and walked over to them.

Hope and Beth soon joined them. "I figured this is where you guys were."

James said, "I just bought me a Harley."

Burt sat on the bike. "You know I used to have one, but it's been a long time."

Dallas tossed him a key. "Take it for a spin if you want to."

Burt grinned and couldn't resist. He put on a helmet and headed down the road. When he came back, he was all smiles.

Beth said, "Oh, I know that look."

James put his hand on Beth's shoulder. "Yep, he just rekindled an old love."

~~~~~

The evening soon came to an end and Sierra and Dallas were finally alone. He slipped his shoes off at the door. He swept her off her feet, "Now I just want you all to myself." He carried her to his bedroom and laid her on his bed. "I'll be right back." He turned on some music and lit a candle.

She watched his every move and wondered what he had in mind for her.

He walked over to the bed and gave her a red rose. He leaned over her face and kissed her as if she were a sleeping princess.

She said, "You know I love the saxophone. Are you trying to seduce me, Mr. Davenport?"

"No, I just want to hold you for a while and feel you breathe." He laid down beside her and held her close. "Sometimes I have to pinch myself 'cause I wonder if you're real, or am I dreaming."

"That's so sweet. How did I get so lucky?"

He lifted her chin to look in her eyes and kissed her. Between kisses he said, "I love you."

She allowed him to touch her at a level they had never done before. She held him so tight and whispered in his ear, "I love you."

"Then stay with me tonight," between kisses, "I just don't want to let you go this time. I want to hold you 'til the sun comes up."

"I'll stay," she whispered. Tears came to her eyes.

"I hope those are happy tears," he wiped away a tear.

"Yes, they are happy tears." They kissed. "I never thought I would find someone like you."

"Well, you found me and I'm yours baby."

They held each other all night as they drifted off to sleep.

The next morning, they didn't make it to church. Sierra cooked breakfast and Dallas took a shower.

"It's a warm sun shiny day, let's take a short ride on the bike," Dallas suggested.

"I want to go home first and shower. I don't want to wear these clothes after sleeping in them."

"Whatever you want, that's fine."

He dressed in blue jeans and a black t-shirt. Before they left, he put on a black leather coat and chaps.

~~~~~

At her cabin, Dallas was singing, and Sierra heard him. "Save a horse, ride a cowboy."

"I'll be right out if you want to go ahead," she peeped out the bedroom door.

He went outside and was sitting on the bike.

She came down the pathway and carried her helmet. She had on sunglasses, her black hair bounced in the sunlight. Her lips were fiery red. To his surprise, she had on a black leather coat and pants with black boots.

He pulled his sunglasses down to get a better look. He couldn't say a word, just kept looking at her and licked his lips.

She got on behind him like she had done it a million times before.

"I'm going to have to lay you down right here looking like that. Lord have mercy," he looked up in the sky.

She just smiled and put on the helmet.

He started to put on his helmet, "I'm gonna' have to go to confession every day this week and I'm not even Catholic."

She held him close and every chance he got he put his hand on her thigh.

~~~~~

That afternoon when they returned, Burt was outside. Sierra jumped off, pulled off the helmet and slung her hair back.

Dallas took off his helmet and he watched her dart up the pathway.

Burt approached him smiling.

"Your niece," he panted, "would make a saint forget his religion." He put the kickstand down and hastily ran up the pathway to get to her.

Burt smiled and tipped his hat.

Dallas pulled his coat off going up the pathway.

~~~~~

Inside he threw the coat on the sofa and pulled his shirt off, throwing it on the floor.

Sierra stood across the room breathing hard, "Daaalllaaasss."

He pulled his boots off at the door, "Sieeeerrrrraaa."

The sofa was between them, and he started around it slowly. She moved slowly in the opposite direction. He changed directions. She made a dart for the door and tried to open it. He leaped over the sofa and held the door shut. He pinned her against the door with his body. She tried to turn around, but he wouldn't let her. He moved her hair from one side of her neck.

He whispered in her ear, "I'm making a citizen's arrest." He placed her hands on the wall and spread her feet apart. "I have to search you." He pulled her coat off.

"What am I being arrested for?"

He kissed the side of her neck. "Premeditated looks to kill." He kissed the back of her neck,

"Illegal use of hands, that's a felony movement violation."

She tried to pull her hands down, he held them on the wall.

"Use of bedroom eyes in the middle of the day." He wrapped his arms around her body. "Attempted murder...to kill my will to be a gentleman." He turned her around and held her face, kissing her. "How do you plead?"

She tried to put her hands around his head. He kept her against the wall with his body and pushed her arms back up against the wall. Both were breathing heavily. Their foreheads touched.

"How do you plead?"

"I'm guilty as charged."

He lifted her off the floor and she wrapped her legs around him. They kissed heavily and fire ran through their bodies.

"What's my sentence?" she gasped for breath.

"Life," he whispered as he rubbed his lips across her cheek.

She whispered in his ear, "How about a compromise?"

He grinned, "Not on the life part?"

~~~~~

A couple of days later Sierra was sitting at the computer when Dallas came in.

"Hey, I want to ask you about these horses," she showed him the wild horses. "Would you go with me to this auction?"

"Yeah, I'm just happy you respect my opinion," he kissed her.

"Of course, I do. I'll make some reservations, it's in July."

He pulled her to her feet and led her to the sofa. "I want you to know something. I've never experienced…the feelings I have when I'm with you," he closed his eyes and lost his words.

She kissed his eye lids. "Me neither, I feel it too." She kissed his lips, "They say it only gets better as time goes by."

"Well, I'm gonna have to pray for strength, 'cause you drive me wild."

"Then I'll pray for strength for the both of us."

~~~~~

Mr. Dabadee and Mr. Cilia heard a rumor that the mysterious girl at Paradise Ranch was Burt Cleveland's niece.

Ari Fletcher was head of security now. He heard a conversation between them.

"I thought we took care of that problem."

"I'll go check public records and see if I can confirm it."

~~~~~

Mr. Dabadee went to the courthouse. Beth happened to be in the vicinity and heard him ask for death records on Abigail Turner.

The girl looked on the computer and said, "I don't have anything. Are you sure you have the right name?"

"I'm sure," he turned and walked away.

~~~~~

When Mr. Dabadee returned to Mr. Cilia, he said, "There is no death record. They've faked her death."

"Mr. Yomosaki is going to need to know about this."
"He's not going to be happy."
Mr. Dabadee called Mr. Yomosaki.
He screamed, "You better take care of this problem!"

~~~~~

Back at the ranch, Landyn had really started causing problems. Sierra's patience was about to run out. Everybody was working.

Sierra looked around. "Where's Landyn?"

Johnny said, "Still in bed, he's been going to the casino at night."

She walked toward his cabin, and everybody followed her. She burst through the door. Landyn got out of bed and started putting his pants on. Sierra held out her hands, "What are you doing? There's work to be done and you're not pulling your share of the load." Her leg began to shake since she was so tired.

"I was getting up to come out there."

"You should have been out there two hours ago. I'm your boss, you show up when I say show up, not when you feel like it."

"You're not my mama."

"She may have brought you into this world, but I'll take you out of it!" She turned to walk away.

"What are you gonna' do with that gimpy leg?"

She stopped and clinched her teeth before she gave him a round house kick in the side of the head, knocking him back into the bed. She hovered over his bed. "That's with my gimpy leg. Do you want to see what the other one will do?"

"No," he held the side of his head.

Everyone's eyes were wide open, and their mouths dropped open. They stepped backward to give her plenty of space to walk through.

~~~~~

That evening, Ari Fletcher come to the ranch. He told them about what he'd overheard.

Beth told them about Mr. Dabadee asking for her death certificate.

Burt said, "We're going to have to be on high alert."

"Great. I had to let Landyn go today. I told him to go work at the casino since he liked it over there so good."

"I heard you knocked him into another realm." Burt folded his arms, "I'm proud of you."

She waved her hands, "It's not like he hadn't been warned."
Ari said, "Maybe Landyn is right where we need him to be."

STAND BY ME

Ari made sure Landyn got a job at the casino by double crossing Anne Roche'. Landyn was informed what he needed to look out for. Landyn agreed to participate to keep from violating his probation.

Anne agreed to pay Landyn under the table.

Ari agreed that Landyn could live in the Turner home place.

~~~~~

Sierra hired three more guys and two girls to keep up with all the work load.

Sierra was resting on the sofa when Dallas came in. He knelt down in the floor, he kissed her, "Do you need Calgon to take you away again?"

"I need..." she placed her forearm over her forehead, "all I need is you."

"I don't like you being tired all the time. It takes away too much energy from us," he rubbed her thighs.

"I have to get things going, then I can slow down," she leaned forward.

"Come on," he helped her up and led her to the bathroom. This time after he ran her bath he undressed her slowly down to her undies.

"I thought you didn't want a relationship based on sex."

He knelt down by the tub and propped his face in his hand, his elbow was on the edge of the tub. He looked at her and tapped his fingers on his cheek, "I did say that didn't I?"

She pouted her lips at him and raised her eyebrows, "You did. I have something for you. There's a box in my closet with a red ribbon on it."

He got up and went to get the box. When he came back, he sat by the tub and opened it. "This is pictures from that day we went riding. I love it."

"I still can't believe a photographer just happened to be there taking pictures."

"These are awesome, you should be a model."

"I wanted you to have some for at your house," she leaned forward to kiss him, and he met her.

"Thank you."

~~~~~

Sierra trained with her horses doing Roman riding with Prince and Duchess. They stayed in sync perfectly, as she had one foot on each horse. Raindancer continued to do well. Sierra noticed how Sprocket had taken up with the horse. Bam-Bam was growing rapidly and seemed to play with Sierra rather than bullfight.

Sierra felt bad in a way for leading Dallas on, then bursting his bubble. She called him. "What are you doing?"

"I'm watching some activity over at the concrete place. Why don't you come down here? Bring the flatbed truck or something. I don't want anybody to see your vehicle."

"Okay, I'm on my way."

~~~~~

She borrowed Beth's car and snuck in the back. "Where are you?" she half whispered.

"In here, don't…"

She turned on the light.

"…turn on the light. Hurry, turn it off," he was looking through a blind.

"Crap! They saw that. He's walking over here. What are we gonna' do?"

"I don't know…pretend sex?"

He sat her on the exam table and started kissing her. She ran her fingers down the blind and started making loud noises. They knocked over a metal bowl and picked it up to do it again.

The man said, "Looks like doc's having a good time," as he walked back to the concrete building.

"That was as cruel as last night," Dallas said as he turned away.

She went to him, "I'm sorry."

He held out both arms, "Where did that come from, pretend sex?"

She held his arms, "I panicked. It just popped in my head. It worked, didn't it?'

He wiped his brow, "Now I need another cold shower."

She giggled.

"Go ahead and laugh. I owe you twice now," he put her in a head lock and gave her a noogie on top of her head. "Look, there's never this much going on at this time of night."

They went to the window, one on each side.

"So, you think they're up to no good?"

"Look, there's the sheriff."

"There's a deputy."

"Yeah, something's going on."

"I can't see," she moved over to the side Dallas was on but was underneath him. "How could we see in there?"

He smelled her hair, "Your hair smells good," he picked up a strand to smell it better.

She slapped at his leg, "Can you be serious for one minute?"

"We can't do anything until they leave."

She raised up, hitting him in the chin with her head. He went flying backward. He knocked over a table and it made a big calamity noise.

She rushed to his side. "Are you okay? I'm so sorry! I didn't know I was that close to you."

She started to laugh and put her hand over her mouth.

He clenched his teeth and rubbed his chin, his eyes widened. "If you were any closer, you would have been inside my jeans." He grabbed her and wrapped his legs around her, putting a wrestling move on her.

She was laughing so hard she couldn't defend herself.

He took full advantage of the opportunity. He took her hair and tickled her nose with it until she begged for mercy. Then he blew on her stomach. They laid in the floor, laughing.

She said, "I love you."

He picked up her hand and blew on it, making a fart noise.

They both started laughing again.

She pulled out her phone, "I need to call James, maybe he can get us some surveillance equipment."

Dallas got up and looked out the window. "There's a big black SUV over there now." He pulled her to her feet. They both looked out the window. A Chinese man came out and got in the SUV.

"I've seen that man at the casino. The driver came to Burt trying to get him to sell out." The sheriff and his deputy came out and left along with the SUV.

She looked at Dallas. "I want in that building. Something's in there and it's not concrete."

He insisted, "You need to let the authorities handle it."

"Dallas, the sheriff is involved. This is the authorities."

He held to her shoulders, "Then we'll go to the DEA or ATF, we'll go over their heads."

"Yeah, but we need some kind of proof to get them interested."

"I've got an idea, but we'll have to wait until they're all gone."

She called James.

"Hey sweetie, what's up?"

"I need some surveillance equipment; do you think you can get some?"

"I've got whatever you could possibly need."

"Awesome," she gave Dallas a thumbs up.

"When do you need it?"

"Right now."

"Alright, I'm headed your way."

They sat and watched patiently until they knew the building was empty. "Come with me." He led her up a steep bank behind the buildings.

"What are we looking for?"

He pointed. "Do you see that unit on top of the building?"

"Yeah."

"Well, what if the A/C broke?" he looked at her.

She cupped her hands around his face. "I knew you were a smart man the first time I laid my eyes on you."

"Stay here, I'll be right back," when he returned, he brought his pistol. They sat having target practice at the A/C unit until they ran out of bullets. "Now the boys can get up there in broad daylight and no one will ever know what we're doing."

"How do you know the guys will get the call?" "They will get the call, they built this building."

They went back in the clinic. Dallas picked up his phone. "Hey Travis. You should get a call tomorrow to fix the A/C over at the concrete building. I just shot it to pieces."

"You're kidding."

"No, we need to get some surveillance equipment in there. James will be here with it tomorrow."

"Okay, so wait 'til James gets here?"

"Yeah."

"Will do."

Sierra said, "Thank you for being supportive. I've waited…"

Dallas put his fingers over her mouth, "Shhh."

~~~~~

Travis got the call to come fix the A/C unit. James went with them and installed the equipment, while the other guys installed the unit.

"What was wrong with the unit?" a man asked Travis.

"Looks like some kid used it for target practice. You're good to go now. Just call if you have trouble with it."

James sat up monitors in the clinic to record everything going on in the building.

Burt, Beth, and Sierra spent a lot of time at the clinic reviewing the activities.

Sierra said to Dallas, "I'm so tired of looking at this screen and all this boring footage."

"Let's take a break and go fishing on the lake. It'll do you some good to relax," he rubbed her shoulders and neck. "I've been wanting some fresh trout anyway."

"Yum, that does sound good."

"It's settled, then. Tomorrow we'll take the canoe, get in a little workout, relax, fish."

"Yay, sounds like fun. I haven't been fishing in a long time."

~~~~~

The next day was spent canoeing on the lake and fishing. They caught a good mess of trout.

That night, they grilled the fish and sat around the fire pit. Dallas and Burt took turns picking the guitar and singing.

Beth said, "We have something to ask of you two." Burt said, "We'd like you both to be in our wedding."

"Oh, absolutely," Sierra hugged them.

Dallas got up to shake his hand. "It would be an honor. Thank you for asking me."

Beth squeezed Burt's hand, "We decided to get married on Paradise Point, but it's going to be a simple wedding."

Burt kissed her, "Then we'll have a small reception afterward."

Sierra looked at Dallas, "I can't wait."

"I'd like to go shopping for your dress Monday. Will that work for you? I already have mine."

"Sure, where do you want to go?"

"I saw some pretty ones in Gainesville when I bought my dress."

"I was going to suggest there, since I lived there. I know where to go."

"Something else, we decided to buy us a motorcycle as a wedding gift to each other. We love to ride and then we can join you guys, James, and Hope."

"Awesome," Dallas said. "That's what's up." He squeezed Sierra close to him and whispered in her ear. She blushed and grinned.

"I heard somebody talk about 'Tail of the Dragon.' It has three hundred and eighteen curves. I'd like to go check it out," Dallas suggested.

"It's a biker's paradise, spectacular views, you'll love it," Burt implied.

~~~~~

Across town, Anne Roche' gave Landyn a job to do. She said, "Don't screw this up or you'll go back to jail. I'll see to it."

~~~~~

The next day, Sierra was awakened by Sprocket crawling out from her covers. He licked her face. He started to bark at the window. Raindancer was outside the window, and he neighed.

"What are you doing out?"

She quickly dressed and took Rain-dancer back to the stable. The other horses neighed when she entered. She saw Diesel and Pebbles playing with the rope pull to the stall.

"Diesel, bad dog. Pebbles, bad kitty." Diesel put his paws across his face. Pebbles ran to the loft.

~~~~~

Sierra and Dallas went to church.

Dylan and Landyn gave their lives to Christ that day.

Sierra thought back to the day she talked to them. She felt overjoyed to have a small part.

"Why don't y'all come over for lunch, we need to celebrate. Just burgers, nothing fancy."

"Sure, we can do that."

~~~~~

"Landyn, I'm sorry I kicked you that day."

"I deserved it, thank you for helping me and giving me a second chance."

"I'm proud you guys made a decision to change your lives. We all deserve second chances and more. God forgives us infinitely. Your salvation is the one thing nobody can ever take away from you. Nothing else matters."

He smiled at her.

"Go see your mama. She will be so happy to know that you two got saved. I'm willing to bet she would love to go to your baptism."

"Yeah, she always said she would 'walk through fire' for us."

"I'm looking forward to meeting her. You tell her, okay?" She waved as they left.

~~~~~

Beth and Sierra went shopping. Beth showed Sierra a dress like hers.

"You need to start thinking about the dress you want," she looked through the dresses.

"Why?" Sierra asked, completely innocent.

She looked at her, "You know you and Dallas were meant for each other."

"We've never even had sex," she whispered.

Beth looked surprised, "You're kidding me. Well, I've seen how he looks at you even when you aren't looking," she held up a gown and put the hanger over her head. Beth pulled her hair out.

"How does he look at me?"

"That man is head over heels in love with you," Beth pushed her in front of a mirror. She looked at Sierra in the mirror, "A blind man could see that he loves you."

Beth grabbed a veil and placed it on her head, "You'll make a beautiful bride."

Sierra smiled at her reflection.

~~~~~

A couple of weeks later, Dylan and Landyn were baptized, and their mom came.

"I want to thank you for all you've done to help my boys."

"They're good boys, I'm glad we were able to help them before it got any worse."

"They told me on Easter, when the preacher talked about Jesus suffering on the cross. They took it really personal."

Sierra listened intensely.

"I've told the boys, but they didn't want to hear it from me."

"But it helped it to sink in, at least you tried," she laid her hand on their mom's shoulder.

"There is no greater love story than what Jesus did for all of us, to suffer and die for the sins of the world."

"Amen," they hugged.

HOT SUMMER NIGHTS

Sierra watched the surveillance video from the weekend. "Dallas, come take a look at this."

They watched the video together.

"Who is that man? He looks familiar," he looked closer.

"Burt will probably know."

"So now we know how they smuggle the drugs in here, but where are they coming from?"

"I'm getting in there tonight," she said sternly.

"What?" he turned his head to look at her. "You're going to get yourself killed, let's just turn this video over to the DEA."

"What if they're involved, how far up does it go? We already know the sheriff is involved. I don't trust anybody on this."

"Let's see if Travis has any ideas how to get in there." He picked up his phone. Minutes later, "Well, no ideas from him."

Later that evening, Dallas had an emergency at a farm.

Sierra snuck into the building right before they closed and found a good hiding spot. She waited and when the coast was clear, she got in to the office. She searched through their files until she found the records that were needed. She took pictures of all of it.

The drugs had been sent in bags of concrete from a limestone plant in Monterrey, Mexico.

When Sierra tried to leave, the door would not open. Dallas was unreachable, so she called Travis to come to her rescue.

"There's a couple of windows up high, but I can't get to them.

Look in the clinic and see if you can find Dallas' repelling rope that he left in there. We'll just have to break the window."

Travis found the rope, by then Dallas showed up. They had two ladders to get over the fence and they broke the window. The rope was lowered, and she climbed up as the two men pulled. "I hope I fit through this window." She grabbed it.

Dallas helped her through the window and onto the ladder.

Once on the other side of the fence, Dallas said, "I hope you learned your lesson."

"I got what I needed," she held up her phone with the pictures. "Thank you, Travis." She hugged him as Dallas coiled up the rope.

Travis pointed to her shoulder, "You're bleeding."

Dallas put down the rope. "Let me see."

"I'm fine, really." She tried to look at her bloody shoulder.

"Let's go clean this up," he led her into the clinic.

~~~~~

"Pull off your shirt," he reached for some gauze. "I don't know what you were thinking, this is crazy."

She pulled off her shirt. "'They killed my parents and I'm going to prove it,' is what I'm thinking." She saw blood drip from his hand. "Let me see your hand. You're bleeding, too."

He held out his hand. "Oh, I'm fine really." He replied sarcastically as he reached for the hydrogen peroxide. He walked up to her.

She looked him in the eyes. "Dallas just believe in me, please. I know you're mad, but I know what I'm doing."

He took a deep breath and nodded, "Turn around."

"If you believe in me then support my decision. And if you promise to love me forever, then give me your hand." She held out her hand and he gave her his. She placed his cut hand on her cut shoulder and held it there.

The energy that surged through their bodies felt like fire and ice running through their veins, as if they were truly one being.

"Now our blood is truly one, our hearts beat as one," she said as they looked deeply in each other's eyes.

~~~~~

Memorial Day weekend was the Grand Opening at the ranch. The black wrought iron sign over the gate said, 'Paradise Ranch- Do Everything in Love.'

James and Beth came to town for the big event.

Chances

"Let's all go zip lining before things get so busy that we can't," James suggested.

It started above the falls going twice over the river. Then you had to walk Lucifer's Ridge to start down the other side.

~~~~~

Back at the concrete plant, Travis was called to fix the window. "Those darn kids must have done it again."

~~~~~

The ranch was a busy place with zip liners and rafting. The water was calm on the ranch but intensified further down the river. The tractors stayed busy with ranch work and taking people to the top of the mountain.

Justin and Chase could barely keep up. "We're going to need another bus," Justin said.

"I'll tell Sierra," replied Chase.

Sierra didn't have much time to work with the animals in the day, so she trained with them at night. Bam-Bam was in the arena, and she moved around him like a pro.

Dallas watched her and shook his head in amazement, then she fell. Bam-Bam walked up to her and licked her face before he turned to run away, kicking as he went. Dallas ran to her aid. Sierra was laughing, "He does that every time," as Dallas helped her to her feet. They walked toward the stable.

"Why are you doing this thing with the bull?" he closed the gate.

"I don't know. I guess it makes me feel like I'm doing it for my dad," she wiped sweat from her brow.

She stood there in a pair of cutoff jeans, boots, and a tank top. He looked at her and wiped his brow, shaking his head.

~~~~~

They walked into the tack room, full of western gear and trick riding saddles.

"Why don't you do trick riding again, I bet you could," he shook a saddle.

She hung up the muleta and swung her leg over the saddle. "I don't have a horse for one thing, and…I guess I'm afraid of hurting my back." She put her arm up in the air and rocked the saddle. "I would rather ride the cowboy," she half whispered.

"That's going to get you in a lot of trouble," he reached for a lasso rope. He wrapped it around her and pulled it taut, both arms were inside. "This is my truth rope, so you have to tell the truth. Do you love me?"

She wiggled and tried not to speak, she clenched her teeth. "Yeeees."

He held her face and acted like he was going to kiss her, "I would lick your face, but it's got bull slobber on it." He kissed her neck.

"That's going to get you in a lot of trouble, mister. Don't start something you can't finish," chills ran all over her.

"Oh, I'm a finisher baby. I'm a finisher." He kept kissing her. Then he tied her hands together, "Come with me."

She got off the saddle and he led her toward the loft. "Are you gonna' untie me?"

~~~~~

Before Burt and Beth's wedding, they all went whitewater rafting. They splashed each other, bounced off rocks, and went down backwards.

Beth said, "Tomorrow at the wedding if you get hot, just remember this cold water."

Sierra rubbed her arms, "Why is it so cold?"

Burt said, "It's at the bottom of the lake, it's not seen sunshine in a long time."

James said, "Sierra, I know you want more horses. I know where you can get some, probably cheap."

"Oh yeah, where?"

"Back in Dallas, a man passed away and his son is selling everything."

"That sounds great, I'll have to check into that."

"Does that mean you don't want to go to Chincoteague Island?" Dallas asked.

She paddled, "No, that just means we would have trail horses that wouldn't have to be trained."

He smiled and paddled. "Alright then, 'cause I'm looking forward to that trip."

Hope and Beth looked at each other. Hope pointed to her ring finger and Beth nodded.

~~~~~

Wedding day arrived for Burt and Beth. The service was at 7:00pm on Paradise Point, with the mountains for the backdrop.

The guys wore black tuxes.

Beth's dress was tea length with lace and sequins all over it. It was short sleeved and ivory.

Sierra's dress was the same, but pastel pink.

Sierra and Dallas kept their eyes on each other the whole time. They listened carefully to what the preacher said.

Sierra felt hot and remembered what Beth said, 'think of the cold.' She imagined it snowing and her thoughts turned to her own wedding. She imagined riding up on a white horse. It was Christmas time with trees full of lights. She could see herself walking up to Dallas and she smiled at him.

"Sierra ... Sierra the ring please."

She was startled and handed over the ring, as she blushed. She looked at Dallas. She knew she was caught daydreaming.

The preacher said, "You may kiss your bride."

Afterward Dallas said, "I wonder where you were during the ceremony,' he wiped his brow. She tried to hide her emotions and thoughts, "I was right there but it was snowing."

~~~~~

The reception was small with the closest family and friends, with dinner and dancing.

On the dance floor Dallas said, "I'd really like to know what you were daydreaming about during the ceremony."

She knew he wasn't going to let it go. She looked into his eyes and stroked his hair on the back of his head. "I was just listening close to what the preacher said. How serious the vows are and what they really mean. They're not just words, you know. They really mean something."

He kissed her. "Yes, they do."

"What were you thinking about the whole time?"

He twirled her on the dance floor. "Mmmm, I can't tell you that."

"That's not fair."

He looked at her, "I was thinking how beautiful you looked with that breeze blowing through your hair and...how hot I was, hoping I didn't pass out.' He hugged her up tight.

~~~~~

The next day they had a motorcycle ride up the Tail of the Dragon planned out.

Again, Sierra wore her black leather ensemble. They were all gathered around the bikes. Dallas said, "Lord give me strength."

They all laughed.

Sierra put her fingers over Dallas' lips.

He bit her finger.

"Ow, he bit me!"

Burt said, "Everybody be careful, increase your following distance."

They all turned to Sierra. "Keep your hands to yourself."

She punched Dallas in the arm. "You kiss and tell." She climbed on behind him and squeezed his waistline to tickle him. He wiggled.

"I was cold," she put on her helmet.

~~~~~

The ride was not disappointing, full of curves and spectacular views.

Sierra held her arms out to the sides, and she felt so free. The day went by quickly and then each couple went separate ways.

~~~~~

Dallas and Sierra returned to the ranch. "I can't believe how cold it gets on a motorcycle when the sun goes down, even in the summertime," she turned on the fire logs.

"It's because we're in the mountains," they held each other in front of the fire. "I've been thinking I need to give you a key to my house just in case. You can go workout any time you want to," he handed her a key.

They started kissing, but it didn't take long to get overheated.

~~~~~

Sierra met Travis, Tyler, and Taylor to look where she wanted the roller coaster. She pointed to the basic layout of how she wanted it to be.

Travis said, "So you own this side of the mountain, too."

She shook her head yes, "But don't tell Dallas okay. I just don't want to tell him yet."

"That's between you and him. Well, at least there's not as many trees to cut on this side."

Ari Fletcher saw Sierra and came outside. "I know Burt's gone on his honeymoon, but a shipment of drugs is coming in tonight. It will be on a semi."

"Hey guys, come over here!" She told them what Ari just told her.

"It's a good thing I swiped the keys when I repaired the

window."

"Oh Travis, I could kiss you!" and she did.

Dallas pulled in about that time and he took a deep breath.

Sierra ran to Dallas and jumped in his arms. She wrapped her legs around him. "You're not going to believe what's happening." She lowered her legs and pulled him by the hand over to the guys.

~~~~~

That night, Sierra staked out the plant from the darkness of the clinic. Dallas got pizza. Sierra watched it all unfold on the monitor, recording all of it.

Dallas said, "I know those wheels are turning in your head, so what are you thinking?"

"Oh, I'm destroying those drugs," she said adamantly.

"You're going to stir up a hornet's nest if you ask me."

"And you're going to help me, 'cause you love me." She pulled him to her and kissed him.

He pushed her away slightly, "I do love you, but have you given any thought to the consequences?"

"Nope, I can't think that far ahead." She took a bite of pizza and fed Dallas a bite.

"I suppose I can't talk you out of it."

"You know they need to be stopped, Dallas."

A semi pulled in and several men were present. They used a forklift to unload the truck.

As soon as the men and truck left, Travis' crew came, and Ari came to stand guard. They worked tirelessly for hours to dump pills with the concrete in a cement truck, and then added water.

Dallas took down their surveillance equipment.

~~~~~

Sierra went home to shower and put on boots, blue jean shorts, and a muscle shirt. She got in her truck and drove back to the plant. When she arrived and entered the building she looked around and said, "Hello. I need some concrete delivered this morning."

"Actually, we have a load ready to go and no order for it. We didn't know what we were going to do with it," the man looked her up and down.

She chewed on her sun glass earpiece. "Great, it's your lucky day then."

Sierra made sure she got the paperwork to connect them with

the concrete delivery.

~~~~~

Burt and Beth came home a couple of days later.

"Y'all are not going to believe what has happened," Sierra chirped as she greeted them. She filled them in.

"You've been busy."

"Yes, we have, and tonight is girls' night out Beth, if you want to go with us. We are going to celebrate."

"Honey, I'm exhausted. I planned to sleep in tomorrow. Another time maybe."

~~~~~

That night the girls were sitting at their table talking rather loudly. Sierra tried not to think about the investigation. She kept her focus on Dallas and it was obvious she was madly in love with him.

Jayda said, "So, when do you think Dallas will propose?"

Sierra crossed her fingers and giggled, "We have a trip planned in July, it's his birthday."

A girl approached their table. "Are y'all talking about Dallas Davenport?"

Pam said, "Maybe, who are you?"

"I just overheard your conversation. He is the sexiest man I know." She turned to walk out.

Pam yelled after her, "Hey! What's your name?"

She kept on walking.

Kate said, "Don't worry about her, Sierra. She has nothing on you."

"She's a has been," Amya added.

But Sierra was worried, and she drank another shot of liquor.

~~~~~

That night she dreamed of a big black bull right in her face. She screamed out in her sleep and woke up in a sweat. Sierra got out of bed and splashed her face with cold water. She tossed and turned and, tried to go back to sleep, but all she could think of was that blonde girl from the bar.

Finally, she got up and got dressed.

~~~~~

She went to the barn early. She didn't notice that the horses didn't neigh when she entered the barn. Sprocket was by her side. Diesel was inside Burt's cabin.

The next thing Sierra knew, she was slammed headfirst against a post. Her head felt like it would explode, and she was very dizzy. She felt helpless.

The man slung her to the ground. He tugged and pulled at her clothes.

She tried to scream, but he put his hand over her mouth. She smelled the same cologne that Dallas liked to wear. She managed to bite him.

"Owwww." He hit her face with his fist.

Sprocket bit his leg and pulled at his pants leg.

Pebbles swiped her claws over his face from the fence above.

The horses pawed at the stall doors.

Sprocket bit his crotch and he screamed.

"You cause too much trouble around here."

Bam-Bam butted the fence down and before the assailant knew what hit him, he was rammed into the wall. He scrambled to his feet and ran with Sprocket chasing after him. Bam-Bam stood over her and licked her face as she lay lifeless.

KEY TO MY HEART

Johnny rushed into the barn and saw Sierra laying there and appeared to be unconscious. "Burt, get down here now!" He ran to her side.

Bam-Bam was standing over her, but he backed away as Johnny approached.

Sprocket and Diesel came bounding through the entryway of the barn and ran to her side.

Johnny leaned over her, "She's unconscious."

Burt ran to the tack room for the first aid kit. He pulled out some smelling salts and broke it apart. He waved it under her nose.

She started to move her head and he held it there again. She moved her arms and partially opened her eyes.

Beth approached with a blanket, "I called 911, they are on the way."

"Come on baby girl, open your eyes," he patted her face. "Johnny, lift up her legs," and he did.

Beth dabbed her bleeding lip with a gauze from the first aid kit.

"Oowwh," she mumbled. She reached up to her head and moaned. Her head had a huge knot on her forehead and a red mark down her cheek. She started to shiver.

Beth covered her with the blanket. "I wish they would hurry."

Burt walked out of the barn when he saw the flashing lights approach.

Soon after the ambulance a sheriff's deputy came down the driveway as well.

"Dallas," she mumbled.

"I'll call him sweetheart," Beth said crouched by Sierra's side.

The EMT Dani asked as she approached Sierra, "So, what happened?"

"She was attacked by someone," Burt said, as he led the EMT to Sierra.

Madison followed close behind with a cervical collar. She placed it around her neck, and then gave her some oxygen. "Can you tell me your name?"

"Abi," she mumbled.

"Can you tell me where you hurt."

"My head," she pointed to her face and tried to pull the oxygen out of her nose.

"You need to leave that in there, it will help you to breathe." They assessed her body for other injuries and got vital signs.

"Here's a pinch in your hand, it's an IV," Dani said.

Burt talked to the deputy. "I don't know what happened, or if she can tell us anything."

Beth said, "Her name is Sierra Wilson, she's 31 years old."

The EMTs placed her on a back board and lifted her to the gurney. "She probably has a concussion since she didn't know her name."

"Dallas," she mumbled again.

Beth grabbed her phone, "I forgot to call Dallas. I'm calling him right now, sweetie." There was no answer.

The EMT's loaded her in the ambulance and Beth got in the front seat. She tried to call Dallas again but got no answer. "He's probably in a dead zone. I'll keep trying."

The deputy said, "Who is this Dallas, she's talking about. Maybe he is the suspect."

"Don't even go there! Dallas loves her, he would never hurt her," he pointed his finger in the deputy's face.

"Dallas, this is Beth. Sierra is okay, but she's been hurt. Meet us at the hospital."

~~~~~

At the hospital, the ER wasn't busy, so Sierra was getting all the attention. It made it look like something was really bad wrong when Dallas arrived. He got off the motorcycle and ran to the ambulance trying to get a look at her. Beth got out and put her hand on his shoulder.

"What happened?" He ran his fingers through his hair. They tried to follow the gurney, but staff kept them out and pulled a curtain.

"Someone attacked her, she has a pretty ugly bump on the head and face. They mashed her lip. I don't think they did anything else," she looked at him.

He rubbed his face. "Did she fight 'em off?"

"I don't know. She was unconscious for about ten minutes after we found her. We don't know how long she was out."

Burt arrived and stood with them, arms folded.

Dallas' hands were on his hips, he turned and punched the wall. He touched his forehead to the wall and put both hands on the wall. He closed his eyes and prayed.

Burt put his hand on his shoulder, Dallas was shaking.

A few minutes later the doctor came out. "Are you with Sierra?"

Beth stepped forward, "Yes."

Dallas turned around. "How bad is she hurt?"

"We're going to get some scans to be on the safe side. She probably has a concussion."

"Can we see her now?" Dallas started into the room not waiting for an answer.

The doctor stepped back, "Go ahead."

Dallas walked over to the bed and held her hand. "I'm here, Baby." He put his lips to her head.

She opened her eyes. "I'm okay. They didn't do anything. It's just a bruise."

Dallas' eyes filled with tears. "It hurts me to see you hurt," he kissed one side of her mouth. His tears fell on her face.

She reached up and wiped them away. "Please don't cry." Her eyes filled with tears. "It hurts me to see you hurt. We are one, remember."

He gave a small snicker.

"Can we come in," Burt and Beth came through the curtain.

Dallas straightened up, but still held her hand. "Sure, come on in."

"Don't make such a fuss, I'm okay, the animals helped me fight him off. He took me by surprise. Pebbles clawed his face, Sprocket got a hunk out of him, Bam-Bam got a piece of the action."

They all started to laugh.

"He wears the same cologne you wear." She looked at Dallas.

"Did he say anything?"

"Oowh, when I bit his finger. Then he hit me in the mouth. He said, 'You cause too much trouble around here.'"

"Did you get a look at his face? What was his build," Burt asked.

"I didn't see his face, but he's white, about my height, and felt muscular. Oh, and his voice is a little raspy."

They came in to take her to x-ray.

Deputy Blanton came in the room, and they told him everything she said and he left.

Burt said, "I don't think that dude believed a word of it."

Dallas said, "She truly is Artemis."

Burt and Beth agreed shaking their heads. "What are the chances?" Beth said.

They all laughed.

Dallas said, "She is a force to be reckoned with, that's for sure."

The doctor came back into the room. "She does have a concussion, but no facial bones are broken. Her spine is okay. Just keep her awake for the next twelve hours. She can take Tylenol, but that's it. The nurse will come in to discharge and you can take her home. She's one lucky lady." He turned to leave.

"Thank you, I really appreciate it," Dallas said as he reached out to shake his hand.

Sierra soon returned to her room where Dallas was waiting for her, "I'm going home to get some clothes and I'm staying with you as long as I need to. Don't even try to talk me out of it." He stroked her hair.

~~~~~

Sierra got out of the truck and even though she was dizzy, she headed straight for the barn.

Beth held her arm. "You really should go straight in the house."

"I have to check on my babies and let them see that I'm alright."

Johnny said, "The animals are fine, a bit flighty, but they're okay."

She petted each horse, dog, cat, and Bam-Bam. "Thank you, Lord, for keeping us safe."

Johnny hugged Sierra and kept his arm around her shoulders.

"At first, I thought Bam-Bam did this to you, then I realized he stood over you to protect you."

"Laying up there in the scan machine I thought, 'How did somebody get a jump on me in my own barn?' The horses let me know something was up when they didn't neigh. My mind was somewhere else that it didn't need to be." Sierra hugged Johnny, "Thank you for looking after us."

~~~~~

Beth joined her sitting on the sofa. "I'm here to tell you, Dallas was scared to death until he knew you were okay."

Sierra tried to smile, but her mouth was getting pretty swollen.

"Let's put some ice on your face," Beth got up to go to the fridge. She handed her the ice pack.

Dallas arrived with a big bag of clothes and set them down in the bedroom. He went straight to her and knelt at her feet and rubbed her legs. "I'm not hurting anything, am I?"

Beth quietly slipped out.

"No, but you can sit by me and just let me lean on you for a while. I just want to feel your body close to mine," she held the ice to her lip and face.

He moved to sit by her.

She laid her head on his shoulder and closed her eyes. She slid her arm under his and they laced their fingers together.

"Doc says you can't go to sleep for twelve hours. I can talk your ears off, or we can watch TV."

"Yeah, let's watch the news. Put it on 13 for Asheville."

Both of their ears perked up when the news team reported six Belgian Melinois dogs were stolen from a training facility. They were the county's dogs to be K-9 officers. "Will you let Sprocket in? I just want to pet him."

He got up and opened the door.

Sprocket was laying by her door. He came in and jumped up beside her and licked her face. Then he curled up beside her and laid his head in her lap.

"I took a few days off until I see you're okay. Travis is staying at the house, and Emily can handle the clinic."

"Thank you. I feel better just having you with me." She laid her head on his shoulder. "Tell me about your family."

"Well, we were raised in a Christian home. We had a good life growing up. My oldest brother became rebellious and caused a lot of problems."

"What did he do?"

"Everything. He said he didn't like having religion shoved down his throat. He did everything he could to go against my dad. That included getting his girlfriend pregnant."

"Travis?"

"Yeah. He was never faithful to her, even after they got married."

"Two wrongs don't make it right. Do you think he ever loved her?"

"She got pregnant with Taylor and then Tyler came along right after that. Dennis said he always felt trapped."

"What about your sisters?"

"Arlene and Darlene are twins, they each had two kids. Julie and Rachel each have a kid."

"Why did you guys decide to come to North Carolina?"

"The boys wanted to start fresh somewhere and said they were tired of living in a meat grinder. Texas was too hot, especially to work outside," he sipped a drink. "A lot of our friends were dying of drug overdoses, and I sure didn't have a reason to stay, so here I am."

"Well, it all brought you to me. Thank God."

"Everything has a purpose, I suppose."

"When my parents died, I felt so alone. My entire life changed. I was mad at God for a long time."

Dallas looked at her. "It all brought you to me." They held each other closer.

They sat there for a while. "Tell me more about Artemis," she said.

He got up to get the laptop. "She was also protector of women and children. She was a force to be reckoned with, most men were afraid of her. She was an excellent hunter and deadly with her bow," he sat there a minute. "Does that sound like anybody you know?"

She rolled her eyes at him and grinned, "Let me see that." She reached for the computer. She read for a while. "She had a stag or dog with her all the time. This says she may have been raped and she may have killed her lover," they looked at each other.

"Do I need to be worried?" he was serious.

She looked at him out of the corner of her eye. "Well, you are my weakness."

He nudged her, "Do I need to be worried?"

"No, she thought the bear was sacred and may have turned people into a bear." They looked around at all of her bear décor. "Okay, this is getting weird." She closed the computer and set it to the side. "The bear is also sacred to the Cherokee and other animals."

He sat there shaking his head in agreement.

"Do you want to watch a video of me when I did trick riding? It has my Mom and Dad on it."

He patted her leg. "I would love to see that."

She put the video in and sat down with him, "This is the night of the accident."

They were quiet as they watched, and he held her hand. When the bullfight came on, it was clear that when she yelled 'NO,' the bull was distracted by her. Dallas hit replay. "Do you see that?"

She watched again more closely, and she turned to look at Dallas. "I have no words."

He looked at her. "I have one word. Artemis."

CAT SCRATCH FEVER

The next morning Sierra looked in the mirror. "I look rough."
Dallas kissed the back of her head. "How do you feel?" He wrapped his arms around her.
"Like I look."
"I would take it all for you, if I could."
"I know you would. I really don't want to sit here again today. I know we need feed. Let's go get some, it will get me out of the house for a little while," she turned to face him.
He put his hands on her shoulders. "Are you sure you're up to it?"
"Yeah, I'll stay hid in the truck. I don't want out in public, just out of the house. Somebody might think you beat me up," she tried to laugh.
"Ha-ha, not in this lifetime."

~~~~~

At the feed store, Sierra saw Landyn. "Landyn, come here!" she motioned with her hand.
He approached her and saw her face. "Damn, what the hell happened to you?"
"Somebody jumped me. You should see what he looks like."
"I'll bet."

"What are you doing here?"

"Buying dog food. Anne Roche' made me go steal some police dogs."

"We saw that on TV. Do you know why?"

"No."

"Where did you take them?"

"Three are in the warehouse across from Dallas' clinic. I took three to an old abandoned farmhouse. She said if I didn't do it, she would make sure I got arrested."

"So, she's blackmailing you. You keep me posted on anything like that. I've got your back, okay."

"Okay, I better get going," he walked away.

~~~~~

When Sierra and Dallas got home, Deputy Blanton from the hospital was talking to Burt. Sierra went in the cabin.

"Dallas, come here!" Burt motioned for him.

"Tell Sierra I went to get some lunch; I'll be back shortly."

~~~~~

Dallas walked into the restaurant, and he looked around. He ordered some food and watched a Deputy Gutman. He fit the description Sierra had given of her assailant. Rage was building inside Dallas like he had never felt before.

Officer Gutman got up and went into the restroom.

Dallas followed him, and before Gutman knew what hit him Dallas shoved his face into the wall. He took him by the neck and dunked his face in the toilet. "Looks like you got cat scratch fever. You need to clean that up." He let him up for air. "Who ordered the hit on Sierra?"

"I don't know," he gasped for air.

"Wrong answer." Dallas shoved his head back in the toilet. "I've got all day to do this. You will tell me who!" He let him up for air and still no answer. He punched him in the gut. "Who?"

"Judge Richburg," he gasped for air.

Dallas kicked him in the mouth and sent him flying backward between the toilet and the wall.

~~~~~

Dallas came home, and Sierra was on the phone. "Hold on for just a minute and I can ask him."

"Hey, will you go with me tomorrow to Dallas to look at these horses?"

He carried the food to the kitchen and looked at her, "Are you sure you're up to it?" He lifted the food out of the bag.

"Yeah, while you're not working. Pleeeeease?"

"If you're sure you'll be up to it."

She smiled. "We'll be there by lunch tomorrow." She sprung up from the chair, "Thank you."

She hugged him. "He has six quarter horses and they're good trail horses."

He had his arms around her. "How can I say no to that face. Do you still want to go to Chincoteague?"

She looked in her box, "I don't know, we'll see."

He looked disappointed. "It might do you some good to get away for a few days." He took a bite.

They went to the table. "Well, it is your birthday. I bet I can't get my money back on the reservations." She took a bite. "You really want to go, don't you?"

"Yeah, I do." He took another bite.

~~~~~

It was late when they got home, and the horses were let out to pasture. Burt, Beth, Johnny, and Dylan helped.

Burt placed his hand on the fence. "Those are some pretty horses."

"I love to watch them run," Beth swung her feet from the fence.

Sierra stood on the lowest rung of the fence. "I'm looking forward to seeing those wild horses on the beach."

Beth turned to look at Dallas and Sierra, "So you decided to go?"

Dallas wrapped his arms around Sierra. "Yeah, we decided on the way back," he lifted her off the fence.

"Dallas didn't give me a choice. He said, 'We're going. End of story.'"

"She needs to learn to listen to me," he swung her around.

"Oh, that makes me dizzy."

He put her down, only to pick her up again. "Right now, I'm taking you in to get some rest."

They all laughed. Beth said, "Young love is so sweet."

Burt pulled her down from the fence. "Old love is pretty sweet, too." He kissed her.

Johnny mumbled something to Dylan as they walked away.

Burt and Beth laughed and kissed again.

~~~~~

Dallas was at work the next day and a pretty, long haired blonde lady came in with a cat.

"I think Miss Kitty may be pregnant, but I'm not sure," she flaunted herself at Dallas as she handed him the cat.

"They usually are." He felt of the cat. "Yep, she's pregnant." He handed her the cat.

"Miss Kitty, you're a naughty girl. I know what you've been doing."

Emily gave her an evil eye as she left.

~~~~~

Sierra went in the barn. "Hey Johnny."

"Hey, you're face looks much better. How are you feeling?" He had one of the new horses.

"My headaches are getting less. I still get dizzy sometimes," she petted the horse.

"You just take it easy, you hear?"

"I thought I might ride this guy over to the other side. I'm tired of being inside."

"I'll saddle him for you." He reached for a saddle, but she helped.

~~~~~

On the way up the mountain she saw several deer. The roller coaster was coming along well. What she couldn't believe was the barren hillside for the ski slopes. All the trees were gone, grading machines were everywhere. "It looks like a bomb has exploded."

She rode a little further down and saw the guys. She waved, "Hey guys!"

Travis helped her off the horse and kissed her head. "I hate they did that to you. We'll get 'em."

She hugged Travis, "I'll be okay. You guys are doing a great job."

"Have you seen the ski slopes?" Tyler asked.

"Yeah, it looks like a bomb went off. I'd like to set off a bomb to Peyton's Place."

Taylor said, "Give 'em enough rope, they'll hang themselves."

"I've got two friends working in there," Sierra said.

Tyler and Taylor stood with her and looked at the casino. Tyler said, "I think they're letting you do all the hard work and then they'll move in for the kill."

She looked at him and patted his face. "How did you get so smart?"

He winked at her.

"I think y'all need to take a break next week, it's too hot. Me and Dallas are taking a trip to the beach for his birthday."

Tyler giggled, "He told us."

Taylor kicked Tyler in the buttocks, and they started goofing off.

"I better go, I'm keeping y'all from working." She was on a steep incline and started to get on the horse, but he moved.

"Let me help you," Travis partially lifted her up.

"Thank you, Travis. I see Ari outside. I'm going to speak to him. I'll see you later." She rode just over the field.

"Hey young lady. I was going to come over tonight, but you saved me a trip," he reached to pet the horse.

"Do you know something good?"

"That same truck comes on the fifteenth of every month to the concrete plant. Tell Burt."

"I will," she turned to leave then stopped. She turned around, "Hey, that truck was from Laredo, Texas, wasn't it?"

"Yeah, but I bet he don't even know what he's hauling."

"The shipment came from Monterrey, Mexico. My question is where do the Chinese bring it into Mexico?"

"It could be any big port, probably a ship," Ari suggested.

"Okay," she waved and rode away.

~~~~~

"I can't wait for this trip, Sprocket." Sierra packed her clothes. She reached for the flowered box, "I can't forget this."

He whimpered.

"Come here, boy. I'll be back soon," she rubbed his ears. "I love you, boy."

~~~~~

It was a long day's drive to get to the island. Dallas and Sierra were equally excited and took turns driving.

Dallas said, "I want to thank you ahead of time."

"For what?" she leaned toward him.

"For making this the best birthday ever," he kissed her hand.

She leaned over further and nibbled his ear and kissed his neck. "Your birthday's not until tomorrow," she whispered.

"We'll never get there if we have to stop and get a room now." He laid his hand on her thigh and squeezed.

"I just wanted a taste," she licked her lips.

He sped up, "You can be a cruel woman sometimes. Did you leave your halo at home this morning?"

She grinned and looked at him out of the corner of her eye. "Actually, I did."

He gasped for breath and shook his head as he exhaled. "Good."

She looked at her watch. "I think we'll have time to walk on the beach after we get there. We're making good time."

He pulled his sunglasses down on his nose and looked over the top of them at her. "Oh yeah, and you may have a fire to put out quick as we get there."

She pouted out her bottom lip and turned up the A/C.

"There's a line down the middle of this car and you need to stay on your side," he grinned at her.

She looked out the side window, leaned back and stretched out. She closed her eyes and thought, 'I won't get any sleep tonight.'

He placed his hand over hers and looked at her lengthy body and long muscular legs. Her long black hair was curled just over her chest. She had chill bumps all over her body. She had on cut off jean shorts and a tank top. He turned the A/C down. He thought, 'I just love looking at her.' He swerved in the road.

The highway patrolman behind him turned on the blue light. Dallas pulled to the side of the interstate.

"License and registration, please." He got closer to Dallas. "Have you been drinking, sir?"

"No, sir."

"You've been swerving for a while."

"I guess I got a little distracted," he pointed to Sierra.

The patrolman shook his head and patted him on the shoulder. "Keep it between the lines son."

"Yes, sir." Dallas exhaled. "I need sunglasses with side blinders." He reached in the back seat for a blanket and covered her up. He began to sing with the music softly and tried not to look at her.

~~~~~

She woke up in Norfolk and they stopped to eat. "Do you want me to drive?"

"No, I'm good. I got food in me and I'm full of energy."

~~~~~

It was almost dark when they pulled into the house. It was a beautiful sunset from their deck. They looked out over the ocean.

"I smell the sea." The breeze blew through her hair.

The wild stallion began to stir. His mane and tail blew in the breeze. His nostrils flared in the moonlight.

Dallas stood behind her with his arms wrapped around her, his face buried in her hair all around him. He started to dance with her slowly.

The herd started to gather. They knew a storm was coming and the journey across the bay.

WILD HORSES

The next morning Dallas woke up to the smell of blueberry pancakes and bacon. Sierra had his coffee already made.

Sierra stood on the deck and watched as the sun started to rise over the ocean. The waves crashed on the shore and the breeze was calm. "The calm before the storm."

Dallas came out in his boxers. "Good morning," he rubbed his eyes.

She turned to the sound of his voice and stepped toward him. "You're just in time to see the sun rise," she took his hand and led him across the deck.

He wasn't looking at the sunrise and they embraced each other. He kissed her forehead and watched for the sunlight to kiss her big brown eyes.

She moved her hands around his neck and pulled him to her. They kissed for a long time. She felt dizzy, like the whole world was spinning around them.

"You've got to kiss and angel good morning and let her know you'll love her all night long," he stopped singing and started to laugh. "I forgot the words. See what you do to me, you make me crazy."

He rubbed noses with her, "That's an angel's face if I've ever seen one."

"Happy Birthday. I hope you're going to wear something besides your birthday suit," she smacked his buttocks and turned to run back inside.

He chased her through the house. He caught her and both of them stumbled onto the bed. "I want my birthday present now," he kissed her. "Then I want another present every hour after that."
"You do? You're not asking for much."
He kissed her all over her body.
"Don't start something you can't finish," she moaned.
"I'm a finisher, I already told you that." He kissed her bottom lip, got off the bed, and pulled her up. "Let's eat breakfast and then we've got to be somewhere by 11:00," he smacked her buttocks.
"Where are we going?"
"It's a surprise. The kitchen."
"You and your surprises," she followed him.
"This smells great, I'm glad you made some food ahead of time," he munched on some bacon.
"I didn't want to spend all of our time going out to get food," she poured him some coffee. "I was afraid you were going to sleep all day."
"Who, me? No, not today." He got a plate.
"And you won't tell me where we're going and what we're doing?"
"Nope," he took a bite.
"How will I know what to wear?"
He thought for a minute. "You're probably gonna' get wet. You're definitely gonna' get wet," he grinned.
She squinted her eyes and ran her tongue over her teeth at him.
"Trust me, baby," he squeezed her hand.
They continued to eat.
"I'll wear a bathing suit under a dress, will that work?"
"That'll work just fine."

~~~~~

Dallas pulled in an area with some small boats.
A man said, "We're not supposed to do this. I can only give you about an hour, maybe less."
Dallas slipped the man some money. They got in his boat and headed into the channel across the bay. He ran the boat onto shore. After they got out, he left.

~~~~~

They ran toward an area that had some brush cover.
The horses were moving all around them.

"I'm not believing this," she held his hand and turned to look at all the horses.

He put his arms around her, he kissed behind her ear. "Look at that one," he pointed to a big black stallion.

The stallion reared up, pawed at the wind and neighed. He watched them from a distance.

"He's letting us know we're on his turf."

The horses continued to gather. They came right up to her, just to be near her. They let her pet them. One mother shook her head as if to say, "Look at my baby," as she nudged a foal that was with her.

They were both in awe of the reaction the horses took to Sierra. They wrapped their arms around each other and kissed like there was no tomorrow.

The horses began to run in a circle around them.

They felt dizzy and their hearts were beating like a drum.

He held her hands. "Sierra, you know how much I love you. I've given you the key to my office and to my house. You hold the key to my heart. Now I'm giving you my heart, because I believe you hold the key to our future." He got down on one knee, "Sierra I believe we are meant to be together forever. Will you marry me?"

"Yes, yes, yes, I love you so much," she was shaking her head yes.

He reached in his pocket and pushed a ring on her finger as he stood up. They kissed again like there was no tomorrow.

There was a boat nearby, with uniformed officers onboard.

"Have you ever seen anything like that?"

The horses continued to circle around them.

"Never," the female officer shook her head.

"Let's get them off the island," the male officer replied.

"Obviously he is proposing, idiot. Keep going. I don't see a thing." They drove away.

Sierra and Dallas only had a short time on the island before the man came to pick them up. Dallas lifted her onto the boat.

~~~~~

When they reached the dock, Dallas handed him some more money. "Thanks, it was perfect."

The man smiled.

The clouds began to roll, and the wind began to blow.

~~~~~

Dallas took his fiancé back to the house and carried her straight to the bedroom. He looked at her, he moved her hair with one hand, as he encircled her.

Sierra's world began to spin. Her dress fell to the floor when he pushed it off her shoulders. He kissed her shoulder. She pulled his shirt up and over his head and tossed it on the floor.

The wind blew harder, and it began to slowly rain. The horses started to move closer together. Hooves pounded the sand.

Sierra traced his muscles. They laced their fingers together and raised their arms. She kissed him and squeezed his hands. She slid her hands down his sides into the V on his abdomen.

Dallas ran his hand up her back to her neck and the bathing suit fell to the floor. He pulled her to him and kissed her open mouth.

The thunder rolled. The waves became bigger, some crashed together as the spray of water burst into the air. Some rolled together, others crashed against the shore. The waves seemed to move in sync with their bodies.

The horses began to run, some on the shore and some in the water. The waves crashed against their bodies. Hooves pounded the sand. Lightning streaked across the sky and thunder rolled. Some horses ran together, and others ran in the opposite direction. The lightning struck and the earth shook as the stallion reared up. The storm lasted into the night.

"I think…we knocked…the earth…off its axis." They laughed and held each other, shaking.

"I'm going…to need a…bigger house," he panted.

"Why?"

"I totally…underestimated…twelve kids."

She stroked his hair, unable to breathe or speak. "I'll…love…you…forever."

The hooves continued to pound the sand.

And the thunder rolled.

~~~~~

The next day the crowd had gathered to watch.

The herd was flighty before they began their trek across the bay. Sierra and Dallas watched from the shore.

The herd made their journey across the bay. They came down the street by their house. Some of the horses stopped in front of Sierra and she petted them as they walked by.

Dallas watched her, "Artemis."

Sierra turned and looked a Dallas. "Did you see that? Come here," she motioned for him.

He joined her and the horses continued to come to them. "They're coming to you, I just smell like you."

"Well, I want you by my side. I want you to experience it with me."

~~~~~

That evening was spent on the beach, and they played in the water. The evening sun was warm, and they laid on the beach holding hands. Dallas rolled to his side and looked at her in a bikini and sunglasses. Her tan skin glistened in the rays of the sun. He began to kiss her stomach and covered her in chill bumps.

She played with his hair. "Don't start something you can't finish."

They could feel their energy surging.

The hooves began to pound the sand and the thunder started to roll. They moved inside before the lightning struck.

~~~~~

The next day the auction took place.

Sierra and Dallas went for a short time just to see the horses. They sat on the bleachers next to a young girl. She was excited.

Sierra asked her, "Are you buying a horse today?"

"Yes, I want to do trick riding."

"Oh, yeah? I used to do that when I was your age."

"Really? Do you know Abigail Turner?"

Sierra was speechless.

"She was a trick rider. I want to be like her."

"Her grandmother used to call her Spirit Dancer."

"Did you know her?"

Sierra smiled. "Yes, I did."

"Cool! Maybe I'll name this horse Spirit Dancer."

"That would be a good name. I always wait to see the horse's personality before I figure out a name."

The girl smiled at her.

~~~~~

"Let's stop here to eat," Dallas said as he pointed to the Wild Horse Saloon and Grill. They had seafood and laughed. They danced some.

Attention seemed to follow them wherever they went. Tonight, the attention was unwelcome as Sierra made her way from the restroom. She was stopped in her tracks when a guy stepped out in front of her. "You need to share some of the action," he said as he grabbed her. "How would you like to be my squaw for tonight?"

Dallas rose to his feet, ready to kill somebody.

Sierra cupped her hands hard over both of his ears at the same time. It sent pain through his body like he'd never felt before. He stumbled backward. She stomped his knee backward.

The man shrieked. "You broke my knee!" The other men rose to their feet. Dallas walked up behind her, ready to fight. Sierra stood with her fist ready to go at the next one. The men backed away with hands in the air. Their friend laid there in agony as they left.

Someone said, "She showed them."

Dallas and Sierra walked out. "That felt good," Sierra said.

"I can't leave you alone for one minute."

She said, "Who's the finisher now?" A fire raged inside them by the time they got home.

The horse hooves pounded the earth, waves crashed, and thunder rolled. Lightning lit up the night sky.

"Those wild horses out there couldn't drag me away from you," he said.

The fire continued to burn.

FIRE INSIDE ME

Dallas and Sierra were sitting on the sofa. "Why don't you come and work some at the clinic? The ranch is running good," he looked at her.

"Beth has been doing a great job and took a huge load off of me. I suppose I could come in a couple of days a week at least. I do miss it."

"I think it would do you some good. Then I could keep my eye on you. I don't want to be away from you for one minute."

"Aw that's sweet of you, but then who would be getting the good out of it? Sounds like it would be for you," she pointed her forefinger into his chest.

"We'll both enjoy it, I think."

"When I first moved here, I thought about building me a clinic somewhere on the ranch."

"That could still be a possibility."

"There's endless possibilities," she smiled.

He squeezed her hand, "What's the possibility we can score a 5.0 on the Richter scale in the next thirty minutes?"

She slipped forward on the sofa and walked behind him.

"Where are you going?"

She leaned over to his ear and whispered, "You'll have to catch me first." Then she ran out of the cabin.

~~~~~

He ran after her and caught her by the river. He panted, "You run…like a deer."

"Well, you caught me, dear. Now what will you do with me," she asked playfully.

It was a hot summer night to make love in the moonlight then cool down in the river. Dallas admired her in the light of the moon as she stood in the river. Her hair cascaded over her body. They heard some brush rustling and then a splash. A large bull elk had walked down to the water's edge to drink, and it saw Sierra. The elk cautiously waded out to her. She slowly reached up and rubbed his nose. Then he turned and went on his way.

"Can you believe that just happened?" she shrieked, as she started to get out of the water.

"I'm not surprised at all."

They sat by the river listening to its tranquil song. "You know the river is sacred to the Cherokee. It signifies cleansing."

"Kind of like getting baptized," Dallas said.

They laid in the field and looked up at the stars while they talked.

"GV GE YU," she said. "That means I love you, or it could mean a few other things like, I will give my life for you, I will surrender my happiness for yours, that you will eat if I do not, you will be safe even if I must put myself in danger, I will protect you with my last breath."

"That's so beautiful. We really should write our own wedding vows, you know. How do you feel about that?"

"We can definitely do that, I love that idea."

"We're having a December or January wedding. I'm not standing there about to pass out again," he swatted at a bug.

"Did you read my mind at Burt and Beth's wedding?" She rolled over and leaned on one elbow.

"You don't want a church wedding?"

"I like it up on that mountain," he laid his hand in the small of her back. "If we're going to have twelve babies we need to get started right away," he tickled her ribs.

She giggled and he kissed her.

"I would marry you right now. This minute. We can go to the magistrate for all I care."

"Can we go to Hawaii on our honeymoon? I've never been."

He kissed her nose, "We can go anywhere you want to go."

She got up from the ground and pulled him up. "Right now,

I'm going inside. The bugs are eating me alive." They held hands back across the pasture.

~~~~~

Kate worked at the casino. She had orders to clean some offices. There was a huge model of the future plans. She took pictures and sent them to Sierra's phone.

"They have a gaundalet going up the canyon," Dallas said amazed.

"That looks like hotels and restaurants and a golf course all over our land. Land was the motive, Dallas." She felt fire run through her body.

~~~~~

Dallas was at work and in came the blonde with her pregnant cat.

Emily said, "Can I help you?"

"Is Dallas here?"

"Dr. Davenport is here," she gave her another evil eye.

She went to the back. "Trip, that blonde is here again with her cat. What do you want me to do with her?"

He cleaned a table. "Why are you saying that?"

Her hands rested on her hips. "She's trouble. I can smell it."

"Awww, bring her to a room."

"I'm staying in the room with y'all." She walked out to get her. "Come on back."

She slung her hair and strutted in her short shorts and high heels. "Heeeyyy, Dallas."

"Hello."

"I would just feel better if you checked on my…cat."

Emily stood with her hands on her hips and tapped her foot.

"Okay." He reached for the cat. He examined it. "She's fine. You'll have babies before you know it."

She stood there provocatively. "Can you keep her until she has them, pleeeeease?" She grabbed his arm as he turned to walk away.

"Um, sure. I guess we can." He looked at Emily with big eyes. "Emily will…um, take care of that." He hurried to leave the room.

Emily put the cat in a container and the lady left.

Dallas peeped from around a door frame. "Is she gone?"

"Yes. I told you she was TROUBLE," she pointed a finger at him.

"How could you tell?"

"A woman knows. She reeked of it."

"Thank you for staying in the room. She was like a tiger in heat." He wiped his brow.

~~~~~

The girls had a night out.

Pam grabbed Sierra's hand. "I want to know how he proposed."

Kate dangled her fingers. "Let me see that rock."

Jayda said, "Tell us about the rest of it, I want to hear the good stuff."

"One at a time, one at a time." She told them about the proposal and all of the horses.

Jayda said again, "Tell us the good stuff. We know you did it."

She smiled. "For some things, there are just no words."

The girls laughed.

Sierra was very serious. "Did y'all feel that earthquake on July 25th?"

"No, what earthquake?" asked Amya.

"We knocked the earth off its axis."

They all laughed again and jumped in their seats.

"There were aftershocks for three days."

"You, naughty girl," Pam smirked.

They kept laughing.

When they stopped, Sierra rolled her eyes to the back of her head. "Do you think my eyes could get stuck back here permanently?"

They burst out laughing again. Everybody was already watching them.

Travis, Taylor, and Tyler saw the girls and walked over. "Can we join y'all?"

Sierra scooted over. "Sure."

Taylor and Tyler grabbed a chair.

Travis sat down by Sierra and kissed her cheek. He held her hand to look at the ring. "It looks prettier on that finger than in the box."

"How long have you known?"

"Um, I think it was New Years," he smiled at her.

She punched his arm.

He winced and grabbed her head to give her a noogie.

"Hey, I want everybody to come over this weekend for a cookout and bonfire. We'll get Johnny to tell some ghost stories."

Kate said, "That sounds like fun. Let me tell y'all something funny. When I took pictures of that model, I had to move it to get the date on the back. I dropped it in the floor, and it broke into a million little pieces."

They all laughed and gave her a high five.

"Good job," Travis said.

"I'll bet that peeved 'em off," Pam said.

Sierra looked at Travis. "Those things are expensive, right?" He laughed, "Aaah, they got lots of money."

~~~~~

A huge bonfire was lit after the cookout and employees, family and friends gathered around.

"Johnny, will you tell us some ghost stories?" Dallas asked. "Tell us about the Raven Mocker and Deer Lady."

"Well, the Deer Lady is beautiful. On her top half she looks like a woman, and on her bottom half she looks like a deer. She dresses in black. You should never look in her eyes, at least not if you are a lustful man."

"Why is that?" Travis asked as he put his arm around Kate.

"You will follow her, and she leads you away and then kills you."

The crowd responded, "Woooo."

Taylor asked, "Who is the Raven Mocker?"

"You never know. They are a witch and just before you die, they take your heart and eat it so they live longer, but there is never a scar."

Sierra said, "Tell them the legend of Nikwasi. That's in Franklin, at the mound."

"Settlements of the Native People were being destroyed and our warriors were losing. A stranger appeared at Nikwasi, and with him many warriors came out of the mound. There was a fierce battle, but the enemy could not see the warriors. The enemy was defeated and the ghost warriors returned to the mound. The next time some enemies came through and wanted to attack, but they had heard of the fierce battle. They tucked their tails between their legs and ran."

"That is super cool!" Taylor said.

"It gives me chill bumps," Tyler shivered.

~~~~~

Emily called Ms. Kitty's owner. "Well, you have six kittens if you want to come and pick them up."

The girl came right after Emily left to get lunch. She was dressed provocatively again. Dallas had no choice but to help her to the car. Dallas handed her the last kitten.

She made sure it landed right in her bosom. She jumped into Dallas' arms. "Thank you."

~~~~~

The next time the girls were together was for the dress fittings.

"I want you girls to wear red since it's a Christmas winter wedding. The evergreens have significance to my Cherokee heritage. So do the colors red and white. The guys will all be in black with red cummerbunds and ties."

Kate gleamed, "Oh that sounds pretty."

"What flowers are you going to use?" Jayda asked.

"Amaryllises, red and white. Christmas trees lit up everywhere," she said as she waved her arm around. "Icicle lights hanging from the trees." Sierra held up a dress. "I think these will be good dance dresses. What do y'all think?"

Moments later, they danced around in the dresses.

Sierra came out in her gown.

"OMG!" Pam shrieked.

"You are gorgeous!" Kate gasped.

Jayda responded, "Dallas is going to love this." Sierra looked in the mirror. "That's the idea."

~~~~~

The roller coaster was finished just in time for fall leaf season. Dallas and Sierra were the first to ride, twisting and turning with their arms in the air.

~~~~~

October was also the time of the Great New Moon Festival.

"This is the beginning of our New Year. There is a lot of dancing," she looked at Dallas and held out her arms. "This is my jingle dress."

"Well, you look awesome. Why do you dance?"

"We dance for everything. To give thanks, to celebrate. In ten days is the Propitiation and Cementation Festival. You can dance then in the Friendship Dance."

"Oh, I don't know about that."

"Then I'll have to get the Deer Lady after you," she kissed him.

"Don't do that! Maybe one little dance won't hurt. For now,

I'm happy to watch you."

The dance lasted until way into the night.

~~~~~

"Hey Dylan, I can't get the four-wheeler started and I need to run over the mountain. Can you take me on your trail bike?" She played with her hair.

He turned off the hose, "I'll show you how."

She put her hand to her cheek. "I don't know, I've never driven one before."

They walked to the bike. "You can ride a bicycle, can't you?"

"Of course."

"Then you can ride this. This is the gas, brake, clutch, gear shift. Easy peasy."

She got on. "I don't know about this."

"Just go down the road," he motioned with his hand.

She kept it in low gear and jerked and sputtered down the driveway. She managed to turn around and stopped by Dylan.

Dylan got on behind her. They made a trip down the driveway with Dylan giving her guidance.

She tried it again alone and started to get the feel of it. She stopped at Dylan again. "Just take me this time, I'll learn it better later." Dylan went with her, helping her along the way.

~~~~~

Dylan went to see Landyn at the casino.

Anne brought Dylan into an office.

"Landyn, we want you to set fire to the barn on Paradise Ranch. You'll be paid good money, but if you don't…well, let's just say you'll wish you had."

Dylan turned to run, but some thugs caught him in the hallway.

~~~~~

Sierra walked down to the casino to meet Dylan. She watched them push him into a van, she recorded it on her phone. She watched them go south.

"Landyn, where are you? Come outside now."

Landyn found Sierra and they got on the motorcycle. "Go to Dallas' clinic." They raced down the highway to the clinic.

~~~~~

She burst into the clinic. "Dallas, I need you!"

He ran out of a room to meet her, "What's going on!"

"They've taken Dylan somewhere. They shoved him into a

van."

"Let's call deputy Blanton."

Landyn said, "I may know where they took him. The dogs are in an old house down there, maybe they took him there."

"Get in the truck. Let's go."

~~~~~

They pulled into an old house in the country. The dogs were inside and so was Dylan, gagged and bound to a chair. Dallas and Landyn broke through the door.

~~~~~

Dylan and Landyn were taken to a hideaway.

Kate and Amya quit working at the casino and went to work at the ranch. Kate was in Sierra's cabin when Travis came over.

"Sierra's not here right now, she should be back soon."

"Maybe I didn't come to see Sierra," Travis said. Travis and Kate kissed in the doorway of Sierra's cabin.

FIGHTING FIRE WITH FIRE

Sierra called James, "Will you come to the ranch. I need your help. I can't get any protection from the sheriff."

"Of course, you know you can count on me," James replied.

Soon afterward, Hope and James arrived at the ranch. He pulled out a punching bag. "You need to get some rage out. Where do you want me to hang it?"

Her eyes glazed in rage. "The barn." Sierra went in her cabin. When she came back out, she had on sweat pants and her fists were taped. She attacked the bag with full force.

They watched her and Burt said, "She's getting ready for a war."

Johnny replied, "Time to warrior up."

Dallas pulled in and walked over to them. Sierra didn't even notice he had arrived and continued to pound the bag. Dallas could feel her rage inside him, he started toward her. James stopped him. "Let her get it out, she needs to clear her mind."

"I've never seen this side of her," he said.

Sierra became exhausted and hugged the bag. She started to cry. Dallas went to her. "I think it's dead. You killed it," he placed his hands on her shoulder gently.

"These people will stop at nothing. None of us are safe. It's not fair!" She kicked the bag and punched it again.

"Let me just make a mental note to myself, to never make you mad."

She snickered a little. "I don't want to feel this way, but I can't help it." They hugged. "I could never hurt you. I would walk through fire for you."

~~~~~

Sierra, Hope and James were eating breakfast. Sierra looked at the paper. "Every time I look in the obits it's full of young people."

James replied, "It's probably drug overdoses."

Sierra got up and stared out the window.

Hope and James looked at each other, then at her. "A penny for your thoughts," James asked.

"This world is turning into Sodom and Gomorrah." She felt the rage building again.

James replied, "A wise man once said, 'My kingdom is no part of this world.'"

"Yeah, and in Isaiah God asked, 'Whom shall I send?' Most of us need a leader," Hope sipped her coffee.

Sierra turned to look at them. "Here am I."

Hope and James sat down their mugs and looked at her.

~~~~~

That night they were awakened by a fiery light in the darkness.

Diesel barked and ran into the barn.

Everyone was scrambling. "Get the horses!"

Duke pawed at his stall door until he broke it and ran out.

Diesel pulled the rope to let Raindancer out. Fire fell all around them. Diesel tried to pull the rope for Prince, but it would not lift the latch. Diesel ran out.

Burt let Duchess out, but she stopped to wait for Prince.

Sierra grabbed Duchess and smacked her hind quarter to make her run. Sierra ran and jumped over some burning beams on her way out.

Prince jumped through the fire and ran after Duchess.

Burt was trapped. He climbed the ladder to the loft. Flames licked at his flesh. He found the loft door. When he opened it, fire flashed through as he hurled himself through the opening.

"Burt! Burt, where are you?" They all screamed.

"He's here!" Beth ran to him, helping him to safety and James helped her.

The fire department arrived and began to hose it down.

"Save the tack room!" Sierra pointed, and she picked up Pebbles. "Where's Sprocket?"

She began to hastily look around, "Sprocket! Come here, boy!

Sprocket!" She heard the sound of ATV's off in the distance.

Sheriff Long showed up at the ranch. Chief Larson motioned for the sheriff to follow him. "You need to see this sheriff."

"What now?" Sierra said as she followed them to the tack room.

The sheriff came to Burt as he was being loaded into the ambulance. "You are under arrest Burt Cleveland, for a massive amount of drugs."

Sierra screamed. "You're crazy, sheriff!"

"There's a huge bag full in there."

Sierra pointed her finger at his nose. "That's planted and you know it!"

He pointed his finger and stepped toward Sierra. "I'll take you to jail, too, for assault on an officer!"

James held her back. "You can't do anything if you're locked up."

She tried to get loose, her teeth clenched. "You just opened a can of whoop ass, sheriff, and I'm gonna shove it down your throat!"

He smiled at her as he got in the car.

~~~~~

Burt was treated for burns to his face and arms and smoke inhalation. He was released to the custody of the sheriff.

Judge Richburg made sure no bond was set and Burt went to jail.

The paper had pictures of the barn on fire, but the headline was 'Former Sheriff Arrested on Drug Charges.'

All the employees quit working at the ranch except Johnny and Kate.

Sprocket never returned.

Beth called the FBI and DEA. All the evidence was turned over to them.

"They are only going to reroute the drugs now."

"What?" Dallas ran his fingers through his hair. "You can't do anything after all the evidence we have against them. This is insane."

One of them said, "We need a good confession to get them on premeditated murder. It was a long time ago."

Sierra stared out at the burned rubble and smoldering ashes. The fire inside her raged. She sat down on the porch steps.

James sat down beside her. "We're going to get 'em, you hear me." He put his arm around her shoulder.

She leaned her head onto his chest, "How can we ever get a confession?"

They looked at each other.

"Fight fire with fire."

She clinched her teeth and took a deep breath.

"I just know they've stolen my dog, of all things."

The agents came outside. "Just lay low for a while. Let the fire die down. I promise we're working on it."

Dallas, Hope, and Beth followed them outside. Dallas sat down beside Sierra. "Faith will test patience." He put his arm around her.

James agreed, "Yes, it does."

"But I've waited sixteen years and they haven't found out near as much as we have in the last nine months," she looked at Dallas.

"When I was a kid, my dad was on his way home from work one night. He stopped to help at a tragic accident. A boy fell over a waterfall and was killed. My dad went to the bottom of the falls and recovered the boy's body. Years later, I grew up and had the chance to help a man. Turned out that man was the boy's father."

All eyes were on James.

"Now what are the chances of that happening? I know you feel discouraged right now. Everything happens in God's time, not ours."

Hope said, "Maybe this scripture will help you from Psalms 51:10. 'Create in me a pure heart, O God.'"

Dallas said, "'And renew a steadfast spirit within me.'"

"Well forgive me, I'm having a hard time keeping a Christian attitude right now. I mean, look at this mess," she threw out her hands.

"Ah, the barn needed to be moved anyway," Beth said. "They kinda' did us a favor. I'm just mad that Burt got hurt. Things could have been much worse, honey."

"I had a lot of good memories in that barn," she squeezed Dallas' hand.

~~~~~

Dallas insisted Sierra go to work at the clinic.

"Hey, is Dallas here?" Ms. Kitty's owner said as she arrived with her many cats.

"He sure is," Emily smiled at her. "Come on back."

The girl waited in a room and in walked Sierra.

"Where's Dallas?"

"Oh, he's busy. What can we do for you?"

"My kittens need their vaccinations."

"We can do that." Sierra checked on all of them and gave the shots. She placed each kitten in the crate. "Anything else we can do for you today?" She clicked her nails on the table.

"No, I'm really disappointed Dallas is busy."

Sierra got about two inches from her nose. "Dallas is taken. Now take your…cats…and don't come back. There are other clinics in town."

The girl tried to back away, but Sierra got closer. "Now scat!"

The girl left in a hurry.

Emily ran to Sierra. "That was hilarious."

"She better not come back either," she folded her arms.

~~~~~

Winter was coming on fast. Travis, Taylor and Tyler went to work on the new stables. Travis and Sierra spent a lot of time together.

Dallas came over and found Travis and Sierra together. Travis was consoling Sierra and she was in tears. Dallas punched Travis right in the mouth.

Sierra got in between them. "What are you doing!"

"You mean, what are you two doing?" He threw some pictures of them together at Travis, who was on the floor bleeding.

Sierra picked up some of the pictures. "I got the same pictures today! That's why we're sitting here and I'm bawling my eyes out!"

"It's pretty obvious to me. How long has this been going on?" He paced and flailed his arms.

"Nothing has happened between us," Travis pleaded.

"Dallas, you know us better than this." She tried to hold his arm. "I love you. We are one, remember?"

He pulled away from her. "Don't touch me." He looked at her and cocked his head. "I should have known you were too good to be true." He walked in her bedroom and took the engagement ring from the nightstand.

Sierra stood with her hand over her mouth, speechless.

He looked at her. "Hell, you never wore it anyway." He walked away.

She sobbed and gasped for air. Her heart broke into a million pieces as she collapsed onto her knees.

Dallas ran to his truck and drove off erratically.

GUARDIAN ANGEL

Sierra desperately reached out to Dallas.

"Dallas, please come and talk to me. You said we would never go to bed angry at each other. I can explain every one of those pictures and it's not what it looks like. I love you and only you. Don't you see somebody set us up. Please call me."

"Dallas, my heart is broken in a million pieces. I know you feel it, too. Our blood is one, our hearts beat as one. Please pick up. I would never cheat on you. I love you so much. Why won't you call me?"

"You gave me your heart and said you would love me forever. Please come back to me. I know a lot of crazy stuff has happened. Maybe you blame me for all of this, I don't know because you won't talk to me. We really need to talk."

"I haven't heard from you in five days. I'm still in love with you and I will always love you. I would walk through fire for you. Please come back to me." Once again, she hung up the phone without an answer.

Sierra saw Travis outside and went on the porch.

"Hey, have you heard from him?"

She shook her head no and wiped away a tear. "Have you," she sniffled.

"No, he won't answer any of our calls."

"Mine either."

"I don't think he's been at work, either."
"How's your mouth?"
"I'm fine, how's your heart?"
"Shattered," her voice trembled.
Travis hugged her. "We're not going to let them win. I'll keep trying to work on him, okay? Even if it means he beats me to a pulp again. You two belong together, he knows it."
"Thank you, Travis." She folded her arms and walked back in the house.
Everywhere she looked she saw Dallas. She wanted to hear something, anything, and she waited two more days. She couldn't bear one more minute in that house.

~~~~~

She ran to the pasture and stopped on the hill. She remembered the night they made love by the river. She couldn't go any further and turned around to see the sun come over the mountain.

In the charred rubble of the barn the only thing left standing was a cross. The sun's rays glowed through the cross, the brightest she had ever seen. She fell to her knees and prayed.

~~~~~

Sierra started to call Dallas and leave one more message, but she hung up without saying a word. "What does it matter now?" She turned her phone off. She looked out the window of an airplane and wiped away her tears. She thought, 'I love Dallas, but I'm not going to beg anyone to love me. I have a mission and I have to see it through. I'm setting you free my love.'

She drifted off to sleep and dreamed of a black bull and white horses.

~~~~~

Once everyone discovered Sierra was gone, Beth called James and Hope. They came immediately to the ranch.

James directed questions to Travis. "Do you guys know where Sierra went?"

"No, she didn't tell us anything."

"Did she ever talk to Dallas?"

"Not that we know of. He won't talk to us either."

"So, nobody has talked to Dallas in a week?"

Travis jumped down from his truck. "He hasn't been to work either."

~~~~~

They all went to Sierra's cabin and looked around. Hope said, "Here's a note on the table!" They all gathered around as Hope began to read the note out loud.

"Please tell everyone I'm sorry and I love you all. Losing Dallas is more pain than I can bear. I have something I have to do. If they are going to ruin my life, I'm not going down without a fight. I'm going to Mexico, don't try to stop me. I chartered a jet at 6:00am and by the time you are reading this, I will be deep in hell. Try not to worry, I know my way out.

Love, Sierra

P.S. I can do all things through Christ who strengthens me."

"I'm going to Dallas' house, who's going with me?" James asked.

"We're all going," Travis replied.

~~~~~

When they arrived, the house was unkempt and he had smashed his guitar against something. Their pictures were scattered. They searched the house.

"He's not here!" Taylor yelled from downstairs.

Tyler yelled from the garage, "His car is gone."

~~~~~

Dallas could see Sierra everywhere. The pain he felt running through his body was unbearable. He realized he did not want to live without her. He was on his way to her house.

~~~~~

When Dallas arrived at the ranch it appeared deserted. He went in her cabin but found no one. He saw her journal laying on the bed but didn't read it.

They all pulled in the driveway. "Look who's here," Beth said.

Dallas came out to meet them.

James expressed openly, "You look like hell."

"Where is she? I have to see her. This week has been hell."

Hope said, "She's gone."

"What do you mean, gone?" Dallas replied.

"She left this morning." James handed him the note. "We just left your house, I thought this might help sort things out."

Dallas read the note and rubbed his head.

James looked at Dallas. "Does that sound like somebody that has been unfaithful to you?"

"No, I want her back. How can we get her back?" Dallas asked James.

Hope held to James. "You better do a whole lot of praying. Only God can help her now."

Travis asked, "What do you think her chances are of getting out alive?"

Beth folded her arms over her chest. "She's the strongest person I know."

Dallas paced, "I never stopped loving her. I just needed time to think."

James said, "Let's pray God will be with her on this journey and bring her home safe."

They all knelt in prayer.

~~~~~

Sierra was getting off the plane in Monterrey. When her feet hit the ground, she felt an overwhelming sense of peace. The pain she had felt all week seemed to dissipate from her body. She looked around as the plane took flight.

"Well Lord, here I am. Now use me to help those that cannot help themselves and for the greater good of mankind." She looked around and approached a man. "Can you tell me where this address is," she showed him a piece of paper.

"It's about five miles from here, follow the railroad tracks." He pointed south.

"Gracias," she started to walk down the tracks with her backpack. The sun beat down on her. She took off her black jacket and stuffed it in the pack. She walked about a mile.

A young man came down the track on a dirt bike and he stopped. "Do you need some help?"

"Yes, I'm going about four miles south."

"That's the limestone plant, bad place."

"Will you take me there?"

"Yes, climb on."

She climbed on behind him. "What do you know about this place?"

"They package drugs into concrete bags and then it goes to America on the train."

"Where do the drugs come from?"

"I don't know." He pulled over. "This place will get you killed. What are you going to do?"

"Sit and watch. I need to get inside." She got off the bike.

He laid the bike down, "You crazy lady, they will kill you."

"How do you know all this?"

"I have brothers that work in the plant."

"Do you think your brothers would help me?"

"Come to my house, we can talk to them tonight."

She reluctantly followed the boy's advice, and they got back on the bike and went to the boy's house.

~~~~~

They pulled into a large farm with Andalusian horses. The boy told his mother who she was and why she was there. The woman looked like she saw a ghost.

"My boys can tell you what you need to know."

That night the young men sat and talked with her.

"Where do the drugs come from?"

"Naucalpan."

"How do they get to Naucalpan?" Sierra asked.

"Chinese."

"Where do the Chinese bring in the drugs?"

"Could be Acapulco, it's a big port."

"Do you know when the next shipment will be?"

"I'll have to do some digging in the office. It might take a few days to find out. If I get caught, they will kill me." Juan looked at her.

Another one said, "They'll kill the whole family."

"Then why are you helping me?"

"Our sister, gray death," Miguel said.

"Gray death?" Sierra felt a sharp pain in her forehead and reached to rub it out.

"She touched raw fentanyl. It killed her instantly," Juan informed her.

"I'm so sorry. What was her name?"

"Dalia, she was twenty-five years old. She died six months ago. You look like her." Several shook their heads in agreement.

There was a turquoise cross necklace laying on the table and Sierra reached and picked it up, as she slid her thumb over the cross, she had a vision appear in her mind. It startled her and she quickly laid the necklace down on the table.

"That was her necklace, and she was wearing it the day she died. She was the one who rode the horses and trained them, her and my dad." Juan said.

Sierra stayed with them and anxiously waited for more information. She wondered why she had a vision when she was holding the necklace. She turned her thoughts to Dallas. She longed to hear from him and the sound of his voice and his laughter. She missed his touch and companionship. She cried herself to sleep.

~~~~~

To pass the time, she went out to the horses. She trained on the horses with the old man. There were three white and three black ones.

Sierra questioned herself, 'I should not be putting this family in danger. They do not need to lose any more of their family.' She decided to catch a train and go to Naucalpan or Acapulco. She slipped out of the house and pushed the boy's dirt bike closer to the tracks. Then she waited for a southbound train.

When the train came, she raced alongside it, tossed in her backpack. Then she stood on the seat and grabbed the bar to an open car and hoisted herself inside.

~~~~~

The train took her to a port in Acapulco. She hid and watched cars being coupled, uncoupled, moved and loaded. There were so may cars, trucks, and vans. She thought, 'How can I tell where the drugs are?' She waited and watched for hours.

"This car is to go to Naucalpan," a man handed a piece of paper to another man, who placed it on the car. The cars had numbers on the sides, and she took a picture. 'I need that piece of paper. What's inside?'

She moved carefully between train cars. She ran behind a loader to get across a roadway. She smelled diesel and grease. She finally reached the piece of paper and took a picture of it. It had the address of a place in Naucalpan, and it was from China.

'How can I be sure it's the right car?' She lifted the handle, slowly opened the door and slipped inside. She pulled out her flashlight and looked around. It was full of raw fentanyl.

She carefully slipped out of the car and closed the door. She saw a ragged tarp and ran to it for cover. Her heart raced, she was sweaty, and the ocean breeze was no relief. She was hungry. 'I hope they move it tonight.' She looked closer at the picture and the delivery date was the next day. She patiently waited and ate a protein bar.

Some trucks pulled in and she heard some men yelling. She peeped out from underneath the tarp and saw men loading girls into a train car. Their hands were tied behind their backs and their mouths were gagged. She sighed as she videoed them. She thought, 'These poor girls are being trafficked.' Fire inside her began to rage.

She decided before dawn to free the girls, even if it meant losing the drug trail. She eased around and sneaked into the car, but she had to hide with the girls when they suddenly came to move the cars. There would be no time for a rescue. 'Will I be able to escape? Now where is the fentanyl car?' The train began to move.

Sierra untied the girls, twelve total. They were from China, Romania, and Russia.

~~~~~

Sierra was able to get the door partially opened, but it had been chained. She pulled out her handgun and shot the chain in two. She climbed on top of the train and found the fentanyl car right behind the girls, it was the last car. Then she shot the chain from the car in front of the girls and opened the door. She found military guns and ammo in huge crates.

Sierra and the girls climbed on top of the moving train and between cars. They passed the ammo and guns to each other until they all reached an empty car further forward and away from the drug car.

When the train stopped in Naucalpan, they carefully made their escape in the dark of the night. They carried the guns and found and old abandoned house to hide in.

~~~~~

Sierra was grateful for the girls, and they were grateful for her.

Two of girls ventured out to find them some food.

Sierra watched the drug house. She needed to see inside, there was a large tree next to the house.

Sierra showed the girls how to make a human pyramid. In the dark of the night, they made their way carefully to the drug house. All the girls made a pyramid underneath the tree just as they had practiced. Then Sierra stepped on the girls to reach the top of the pyramid. Sierra reached for a strong limb and sat videoing the drug activity through the window.

There were gas tanks everywhere in the house and Sierra decided as the train pulled away to blow up the house with the RPGs they stole from the train.

The girls continued to watch from their hideout.

It took a few days for the shipment to be ready and loaded back onto the train car.

When the train stopped the girls were ready with military precision. They had to sneak back onto the train and carry the guns and ammo.

The train began to pull away and Sierra had the RPG ready and fired directly into the drug house. There were multiple large explosions when the gas tanks began to explode.

The girls gave each other high fives and hugged each other. Sierra knew someone would be looking for the ammo and the girls. Now they would be looking for whoever blew up their drug house.

~~~~~

When the train stopped outside Monterrey, the girls all jumped off. They headed to the ranch where all the guys were. The girls carried huge bags full of money that was on the drug car. They stayed at the ranch a few days.

Juan was able to get the evidence Sierra needed. The shipment was going to the trucking company in Laredo. He got video of a politician from Texas. Juan switched a shipment of concrete with the drugs and sent the drugs to the DEA building in Laredo.

"I want your family to have this money. I can't thank you and your family enough," she hugged Juan.

"You've helped us a lot, we thank you."

~~~~~

That night, they set dynamite and blew up the limestone plant.

~~~~~

They danced and celebrated into the night.

Sierra was exhausted and she didn't know how she was going to get home or what to do with the girls. She leaned against a wall and thought of Artemis, protector of women.

Juan approached her and began to play with her hair. "Stay, you don't have to leave."

"I've been gone for two weeks. My family will be worried sick."

"We're having a bullfight tomorrow, at least stay tomorrow. We'll get you home," he leaned in to kiss her.

She turned away. "I can't. I'm in love with someone."

He looked down and sighed, "I understand. He's a lucky guy," Juan said.

The next day everyone was gathered to watch the bullfight.

The old bull was a huge Spanish bull. It reminded Sierra of the bull she would see in her dreams.

A couple of the guys went out to bullfight. Others were close by to distract the bull. The bull charged suddenly, and a man was thrown. The other man was twirling around with the muleta, he narrowly escaped a goring. Then it happened. He was down. The bull pounded him against the ground.

It was the meanest bull she had ever seen.

Without hesitation Sierra ran out, grabbed the muleta and distracted the bull until they got the man out of harm's way. She stood there glaring into the bull's eyes and clinched her teeth and scowled at him. He snorted and pawed at the ground. He glared back at her, as if to size her up. She bowed her head and said softly "Satan I expose you as a spirit of fear in my life and I bind that fear in Jesus' name." He stepped backward. She lifted her head and took a step toward him and held her shoulders back. He snorted and charged at her. She screamed "Satan get behind me", as she spun around him time and again.

The crowd cheered as the bull exited the arena.

Sierra felt like she had just danced with the devil and defeated him.

~~~~~

Back home Dallas saw Sierra's journal and this time he picked it up and began to read.

Dec 26- Today I helped bring new life into this world. I feel much pride and hope that Dad would be proud of me. In doing so, I met someone special. I have to wonder if there was some divine intervention, or maybe he was sent by Mom and Dad. Anyway, he seems to be sent from Heaven. When I look in his blue eyes all see is Heaven. Surely, he is an angel.

Dec 27- It's so hard to concentrate on the ranch. My mind continuously wanders off to Dallas and the many questions I have about him.

Dec 28- I can't wait for my date with Dallas. He's so hot. I want to run my fingers through his wavy black hair and linger on his luscious lips.

Dec 30- Dallas called me tonight and we talked a long time. He's looking forward to our date, too. I'm so nervous but at the same time I feel like I'm at home with him. I want it to be perfect.

Jan 1- I think today is the first day of the rest of my life. The way Dallas makes me feel is incredible and sometimes I have to remind myself to breathe. Dancing with him and feeling his body next to me made it feel like I was high or something. And then there was the kiss. I thought electricity was running through my body. I began to shake and felt my temperature go to 1000 degrees. I know he thought I was cold, but I was literally on fire. At home, he made me feel the same way and I love the way he pulls me to him.

January- Dallas came to see me unexpectedly today. I think he used the calf for an excuse, but I'm glad he did. We played around and up in the loft, he really let me know he is attracted to me, too. He has an awesome body. He is so sexy. I felt so weak and helpless with his touch and I really didn't care. How could someone I just met make me feel so vulnerable and out of control.

Dallas flipped pages to Valentine's Day.

Feb 14- For the first time in my life, I'm looking forward to Valentine's Day. I think I'm in love with Dallas. It seems crazy, only knowing him for two months, but I can't help it. I really think I would walk through fire for him. I long to be with him every minute.

Dallas flipped over to March.

March 21- I spent the night with Dallas last night for the first time at his house. He asked me to, and I could not resist. I loved being wrapped in his arms and feeling his body next to me all night. His breath on my face was like having and angel breathe on me all night. I felt safe and like I belonged there. I would love to wake up next to him every day.

June- Dallas has no idea how much money I'm worth and I don't want him to know. I know he is suspicious of something. I've always had a fear that someone would just want me for my money, but I'm certain that he loves me for me, right down to my soul.

June- Today, I pledged myself and my love forever to Dallas. We both were cut and I saw an opportunity to join our blood truly as one. I know he doesn't understand yet, the bond that is between us can't be broken.

July- I hope Dallas is going to ask me to be his wife. I can't imagine my life without him. I think the biggest thing that attracted me to him is that he is a Godly man. There's just no other explanation.
Thank you, God, for Dallas and the unconditional love that we share.

July 25- At Chincoteague Island, Dallas proposed to me today. I think the horses even blessed us, or God one. Either way, it doesn't matter. Making love to Dallas for the first time was the most amazing experience I've ever had. There are literally no words to explain. I think the closest I can say would be that we knocked the earth off its axis. The love I feel for him cannot be measured. I know God made him just for me.

July- I know Kate and Travis hooked up last night. I hope they can have love like we do. I never knew love could be so awesome. Kate and Travis are both deserving of true love.

August- Today I asked Travis about the blonde in the restaurant, and she used to be Dallas' girlfriend. Her name is Lana. Travis said Dallas never loved her or even came close to what he and I have. Knowing that makes me feel so much better. I don't know why, but it does. I should have never let her enter my mind or bother my thoughts. I know when I was attacked that's what I was thinking about.

'Holy moly, I can't believe this. I wish she would have just asked me. I should not be reading this,' Dallas thought, as he flipped to the last entry.

My heart is broken into a million pieces. I don't know how I'll ever be able to put my life back together again. Without Dallas, I just don't care anymore. If I could say one thing to Dallas right now, it would be this. I prayed for you, God will surely bring you back to me.

He closed the journal and ran his fingers through his hair.

RETURNING HOME

Dallas tried to work, but his mind was solely on Sierra. 'Our blood is one, our hearts beat as one,' repeated in his head over and over.

Beth called Dallas, "We just received Sierra's passport via FedEx. She left it on the plane. She hasn't had it the whole time."

"How will she get back in the U.S.?"

"I don't know."

"Then I'm going after her." He ran out the door.

~~~~~

Dallas went to get Sierra's passport. "Johnny, where are you going?"

He was dressed in camo and his face was painted. "To find Sprocket. That's the least I can do to help Sierra. Time to warrior up."

"Let me ask you something. Sierra and I were both cut, and somehow, I don't understand she joined our blood together. She said our blood is one and our hearts beat as one. What does all that mean?" He looked up at Johnny on the horse.

Johnny looked down and sighed, then he dismounted the horse. "That's a blood oath, it was sacred to her. She pledged herself to you forever," he paused. "Did you tell her you would love her forever?"

"Yes."

"Did you willingly give your blood?"

"Yes."

"It's an old custom, but it obviously means something special to her."

Dallas raised his eyebrows. "Wow."

Johnny pointed his finger at his heart. "Do you feel her? Open your mind, feel her spirit in you. She is leading you out of the darkness, because you did that for her. We are all spiritual beings having a human experience. You must find your true self through the hardships in this life. There are lessons with all those hardships. Forget about material things, your career and social status. That is not who you truly are. Going to church does not make you a spiritual person. You must learn to release the things that no longer serve you. Then you can follow the light inside of you, that is God's love. His love for us will never die, just as the love we have for the one's we have lost. That love is in us." He mounted the horse and trotted away.

~~~~~

Officer Gutman escorted Burt into an interrogation room. Deputy Blanton saw them go in and Sheriff Long a few minutes later. When Officer Gutman came out Deputy Blanton was ready. His upper cut was so hard it knocked him out cold, in a heap in the corner.

The sheriff cocked one hip onto the table and asked, "Where is that little niece of yours? Yeah, I know that's your niece back from the dead."

"How would I know? I'm stuck in here," he looked at the sheriff and held up his handcuffed hands. "I wouldn't tell you if I did know."

"She's somewhere causing trouble. I know because we didn't get our goods."

Burt smirked at him.

He punched Burt in the mouth.

"It's too bad about your sister. I never meant for her to die. When that semi hit 'em, I guess they didn't have a chance in hell."

Burt glared his eyes at him and clinched his teeth.

"Yeah…I was the trigger man. It would've been simple if they would have just sold out, or if that bull would've gotten Tom at the rodeo. You got more land than you know what to do with."

"You're gonna' rot in hell," Burt spat on him.

He wiped his face. "Now that niece of yours, she knows what

she's doing. I'll take care of her when she gets back in town." He stood up and walked out of the room.

When the sheriff came out of the room he was face to face with Deputy Blanton. Blanton punched him, knocking him out. He looked at Burt, "I recorded the whole thing."

Burt was released and the SBI and IA arrested Sheriff Long and Officer Gutman.

~~~~~

The news traveled fast in the small town. The community rallied behind the former sheriff and ranch and all the workers returned. Triple T construction had multiple helpers to rebuild the stables.

~~~~~

Dallas flew to Monterrey. He started showing pictures of Sierra to people at the airport.

"She was here about two weeks ago. She wanted to know where the concrete plant was. It's blown to pieces now."

"Can I borrow a vehicle?"

"Take my old truck," he handed him the keys. "It's five miles south of here."

~~~~~

Dallas drove the truck to the site of the plant and saw the chaos. He stopped at the edge of the road. The boy on the motorcycle was sitting there watching.

Dallas approached the boy, "Have you seen this girl?" he held out his phone.

"Who are you?"

"She's my girlfriend and I need to find her. I think she may be in trouble."

"Yeah, I've seen her. She's been to my house. We helped her."

"Where is she now?"

"She left on the train yesterday."

"Where was she going?"

"Laredo."

"Thanks man," he got back in the truck.

~~~~~

Sierra, all the girls and six horses were on board the train. They hid in the hay with the horses around them.

There were men on the train looking for anybody they suspected ruined their goods.

Sierra watched the men question the passengers and then she got up and moved through some of the passenger cars. She headed back to the girls on the livestock car. In her haste the clothing she had around her slipped and fell to the ground.

One of the men took notice and followed her.

Sierra's expression was clear even if the girls didn't really understand her. "We have to get off the train. Bad men are looking for us."

Suddenly one of the men burst into the car. Sierra turned around and began punching and kicking him. He fought her back. The girls all jumped on him and held him down. They pulled off his clothes hogtied him, and then threw him off the train in the middle of nowhere.

Sierra tried to uncouple the train car but could not get it to budge. She looked for something to knock it out of the locking system. She looked around and found an ax at the end of the car.

One of the men saw her just as she swung the ax and freed the fated car from the train.

Sierra's intuition told her they had a very small window to escape and get as far away from the train car as possible.

She loosened the loading ramp and shoved it to the ground. Each horse was carefully led down the ramp and handed to the girls.

They helped each other get on the horses. There were no saddles. They would have to ride bareback.

Just as the fifth horse stepped off the ramp, the ramp crashed to the ground. The horse was spooked but Sierra held to the reins tight.

One horse remained on the car.

Sierra squeezed the bridge of her nose between her fingers and squeezed her eyes shut, 'No way I'm leaving one behind,' she thought.

She hoisted herself into the car and wiped the sweat from her brow. She climbed onto the back of the horse and walked it around in the car briefly. She walked the horse to the edge of the platform and the horse stopped and backed away.

The girls eagerly watched to see what Sierra would do next.

Sierra again walked the horse to the edge of the platform, and it backed away. Again, she walked the horse around in the car faster. She clutched the hair of his mane, kicked him hard in the ribs with her heels and sailed off the platform to their freedom.

~~~~~

The girls began their treacherous journey through the desert. They guessed at which way Laredo was by the direction of the tracks and watching the sun as it began to set.

Her intuition proved to be right when she heard motorcycles and vehicles.

The girls looked at Sierra and tried to communicate.

Sierra took a deep breath and exhaled. She motioned for them to follow her as she nudged her horse in the ribs to break into a run. They ran across the desert.

Sierra headed for a ravine where the terrain became rocky making it impossible for the enemy to follow. It also made it difficult for the horses and girls. Sierra could see no other way.

"We need to rest," one of the girls said.

"Okay, just a little while."

The girls helped each other to dismount the horses. They sat down on the rocks and comforted each other. They had no food and no water. They watched their fearless leader kneel down on her knee and began to pray.

Although they had difficulty communicating to say the least, the girls gathered around Sierra. The youngest girl reached for Sierra's hand.

Sierra opened her eyes and looked at the fear on their faces. She knew she had to remain strong. And in that moment, she knew she was right where God needed her to be.

Sierra began to say the 23rd Psalm out loud.

"The Lord is my shepherd; I shall not want. He maketh me to lie down in green pastures: he leadeth me beside the still waters. He restoreth my soul: he leadeth me in the paths of righteousness for his name's sake. Yea, though I walk through the valley of the shadow of death, I will fear no evil: for thou art with me; thy rod and thy staff the comfort me. Thou preparest a table before me in the presence of mine enemies: thou anointest my head with oil; my cup runneth over. Surely goodness and mercy shall follow me all the days of my life: and I will dwell in the house of the Lord forever. Amen."

The heat from the day made the clouds gather and it began to get dark. They could hear the thunder roll and then the rain began to fall steadily. Sierra stood and held out her arms and looked to the heavens. "Thank you, Lord."

They were cold and wet, but the rain was a gift from above. The girls huddled together to stay warm as the night fell upon them.

Sierra woke the girls, "We have to go now. If we can just get to the river, we're home."

The girls mounted the horses and eased toward the opening of the ravine.

The men were waiting patiently for them and this time they had a chopper.

When Sierra heard the whine of the engine increase, and the blades begin to beat the air she slid down off her horse. "Give me that last RPG!" She reached for it. "Time to meet your maker or burn in hell!" She held tight and braced herself. She fired, blowing the helicopter from the sky.

"We have to make a run for the border now!" She tossed the weapon, mounted her horse and whistled for the horses to follow her. They headed for the Rio Grande with the other men in pursuit.

Over the ridge a large herd of horses came from out of nowhere. They stampeded toward the girls and surrounded them.

The men couldn't see the girls mixed with all the horses.

The herd seemed to guide them as they ran through the desert terrain and straight to the river.

They were met by ICE agents outside Laredo and just over the border. They were taken into custody and the horses were loaded on a trailer.

~~~~~

"What's your story young lady?" an agent asked at a desk.

"I rescued these girls in Acapulco.

"Where are you from?"

"I'm a U.S. citizen."

"Where's your passport?"

"I've lost it."

"What's your name?"

"Sierra Wilson." She waited.

"There's nothing to confirm who you are, you are going to have to remain in custody." An agent started to handcuff her.

"Wait, wait. I'm a member of the Eastern Band of Cherokee Indians. They know me as Abigail Diana Turner, daughter of

Diana Gayle and Tom Turner. Call them, they will confirm it," she pleaded.

She paced and waited anxiously.

The agent returned. "Well, you do check out. You're free to go."

"Thank you. Can you take me to my horses please? First, I need to call home, give me just one minute."

"Beth, it's Sierra. I'm in Texas and I'm on my way home. I'll try to call you back later, sorry I had to leave a message." She hung up.

Sierra and the girls said their goodbyes and hugged. "Be strong, warrior up." She posed her arms, to show strength.

~~~~~

Dallas reached the ICE office. "I'm looking for a girl that might have come through here."

"What's the name?" the agent asked.

"Sierra Wilson," he leaned on the counter.

"Nobody came through by that name," the woman looked on the computer.

"Are you sure?" He pounded his fist on the counter.

"Positive."

He walked away from the counter.

Beth called Dallas. "Sierra called. She's on her way, so come home."

"Where is she?"

"I don't know, somewhere in Texas. She left a message, but she's on her way."

"Thank God."

MENDING FENCES

The ICE agents took Sierra to a ranch outside of Laredo.

"Hi," Sierra greeted an older man. "These are my horses and I need help to get them to North Carolina. Do you know anybody that would be willing to drive it?" She had one hand on a hip and one on her brow.

"Let me make some calls and I'll see what we can do," the man picked up his phone.

"Thanks. I'll pay them good money."

"If we can't find somebody, you could take the train."

"No, no, no more trains. I'm sick of trains," she held up her hands.

He scratched his head and continued to make some calls, but no luck.

Sierra chewed a broken nail. "Do you have anything I can eat? I don't remember when I've eaten last. I'm feeling kinda' sick."

The man said, "Come in the house," he motioned for her to follow him. "My wife will find you something."

The woman fixed her a plate of BBQ, beans, slaw, and hush puppies. She stuffed it in. "Oh my gosh, this is so good. Thank you so much."

They watched her eat. "How did you end up in this predicament?"

"If I told you, you'd never believe me," she continued to eat.

The woman asked her husband, "Have you tried to call DC?"

"No, I haven't." He picked up the phone.

"DC, I've got a situation...This young lady needs to get back to

North Carolina and she has six horses...She doesn't want to get on a train, that's what I suggested. Well think about it quick and call me back." He looked at his wife and they both crossed their fingers.

The phone rang a few minutes later.

"Yeah...You'll do it?...That's great!...She wants to get on the road tonight if at all possible...

Okay, see you shortly." He hung up.

"You are in luck today young lady. This man will take good care of you, and you can trust him. We call him DC and I've known him a long time."

"Thank you so much, you're a God send. So is this DC."

The woman said, "God works in mysterious ways."

"Maybe you're the God send," the man added.

"Do you have a business card or something so I can keep in touch with you guys?"

"Sure," the woman handed her one. DC pulled in about thirty minutes later with a big truck and horse trailer. The man said, "I didn't even catch your name, little lady."

"Abi," she reached to shake hands with DC.

"Are you ready for a road trip?"

"I can't wait to get home. I've been gone almost three weeks."

DC started loading the horses on his trailer. "You've sure got some pretty horses."

Sierra led some horses. "Yes, they are."

"I just ask one thing."

She looked at DC. "What's that?"

"None of this crazy hip hop, rapping stuff on the radio."

She laughed. "Deal," they fist bumped.

"We'll head north on 35, hit 30 in Dallas and take 40 the rest of the way. Does that sound like a plan?"

"Yeah," she shook her head and smiled. "I can help drive, too."

"Alright North Carolina, here we come. How in the world did you wind up here?"

"It's a long story."

"It's a long ride, sweetheart."

"Can I use your phone to call somebody? Mine broke. Then I'll tell you all about it."

She tried to call Dallas, but no answer. "I'll try again later.

Well, I started in Monterrey.... That's how I ended up in Laredo."

"So, that big explosion in Mexico City and Monterrey, was you?"

"Yep."

"I saw it on the news. Hell, NASA saw it from the space station."

"Really," she grinned. "Somebody had to put a stop to it."

"No wonder they were after you, they meant to kill you." He looked at her.

"Yes, sir, they did. I guess I worked my guardian angels overtime. It was strange how I had no plan at all, and God provided a way so many times," she looked out the window at Dallas, Texas. She was quiet the whole way through, she thought of Dallas. She tried to call him again, still no answer.

"You play the same kind of music my fiancé listens to. He sings to me all the time," she started to choke up. "Except he's not my fiancé anymore."

"Why? What happened?"

"We had a fight...he took the ring back and I left town. He thought I cheated on him, but I didn't."

"That sort of thing can cause a lot of problems. It can tear a family apart."

"Yeah, a lot of things can. Prayer can change a lot of things, too." She looked at him. "Someday I might forgive these people, I know unforgiveness will make you miserable and consume you till there's nothing left but a shell."

"I guess we all have some skeletons in our closet. I know I do."

"Can we stop at this exit, please? I'll drive a while if you want me to."

"Why don't you take a nap, then we can switch off. You look beat."

"I am. I slept on a rock in the desert last night, after I got rained on. I know I stink," she smelled her shirt. "Yep."

When they returned to the truck DC said, "There's a pillow and blanket in the back."

She reached for it and placed it under her head, "Wake me up if you need me." She thought, 'It smells like Dallas,' and she drifted off to sleep.

Hours later she woke up. "That was amazing. I can't believe you let me sleep that long. Where are we?"

"Just went through Memphis."

"I've heard all over hell in half of Georgia, but I think Texas has 'em beat."

"I'll agree with that one. Are you hungry?" he rubbed his tummy.

"Starving."

"The horses could use something, too."

~~~~~

They tended to the horses, went to a Waffle House, and got fuel.

Sierra got in the driver's seat, "Wow, this is big."

"Are you sure you can handle this thing," DC asked.

"Oh yeah, no problem. It's longer and wider than mine, but I should be okay."

~~~~~

After DC felt comfortable with her driving, he said, "I'm going to close my eyes a while. My eye balls are starting to run into the same hole."

She laughed. "I got this, straight ahead, just hold it between the lines."

She stopped in Lake Junaluska for fuel and DC woke up. They grabbed food to go and ate in the truck. DC got in the driver's seat.

"We're on the home stretch now," Sierra said.

"Yep, it's beautiful here," he looked out over the mountains.

She picked up his phone. Dallas still wouldn't answer. "Beth, I'm in Lake Junaluska so I'll be there in about an hour. Love you."

"People stay on the phone, but they never answer when you really need 'em to."

"They stay so busy. We don't keep our phones on us constantly. I know I don't. With everything that's happened I just don't know what to expect when I get there."

"I wish you nothing but the best, young lady. I hope that fella' of yours comes to his senses. From what I can gather, you are one of a kind."

"Thank you, thank you for all of it. When we get there, I'll write you a check or I'll pay you in cash, which ever one you want."

"I needed to come to North Carolina. I have family here I've not seen in a while. I'm actually looking forward to seeing them."

"Why didn't you tell me?"

"It wouldn't have changed anything, we still had to come."

Chances

She looked at him and smiled. "Yeah, I guess. Turn left at the light on Seven Clan's Road. Just a couple more turns, and we'll be there."

~~~~~

They turned down the driveway.

"Oh my gosh, who are all these people? The barn is built. I can't believe it. There is my uncle!" As they got closer, she could see a "Welcome Home" sign hung on the side of the barn.

"Stop, stop the truck! There's Dallas!" Her heart pounded. She got out of the truck and started to run to him, then she stopped. He saw her and they looked at each other. She was filled with every possible emotion imaginable. Both of them ran to each other and embraced. He lifted her off the ground and swung her around. They kissed. Everyone clapped and cheered.

Dallas' face was covered underneath her hair. "I love you. I'm so sorry I ever doubted you."

"I love you, too."

"Please forgive me."

"I did a long time ago. I told you I would love you forever," she kissed him.

Burt and Beth came over and hugged Sierra, followed by James, Hope and Johnny. Then she wrapped her arms around Dallas again.

Dallas said, "I can't believe you made it, but why is there a horse trailer?"

"Oh, where are my manners." She ran and opened the door for DC to get out. "DC, this is my family and my home." Everyone was watching. DC got out and looked at Dallas. Dallas looked shocked. There was complete silence.

"Do they know each other?" someone asked in the crowd.

Dallas said, "That's my brother."

The two men walked up to each other and embraced.

"Dad!" Travis, Tyler and Taylor ran to their dad and joined in a group hug.

"Thank you for bringing the love of my life back to me," Dallas said.

"She's quite a catch, you better hold on to her."

Sierra watched the guys as she wiped away some tears. "I didn't know it the whole trip." She joined the group hug.

"I thought you were mad at me for punching Travis and that's why you were calling."

Sierra said, "That was me calling you."

"It showed up as Dennis," Dallas said.

"I thought your girls name was Sierra," DC was confused.

"I told DC my name was Abi. ICE held me without my passport. I had to tell them I was Abigail Turner and to call the EBCI to get back in the U.S."

"I was at the ICE agency in Laredo and asked for Sierra Wilson."

"What?" She held his arm. "You came after me?"

"Yeah, I flew to Monterrey and saw where you had been, nice job. Some kid on a motorcycle told me where you were. Then I went to Laredo and…"

"What day and time?"

"Probably 10:00am the day before yesterday."

"We just missed each other."

Dallas said, "What are the chances?"

"This is all crazy," Travis said.

They all sat around and talked for hours, telling stories and looking at the barn and horses. Burt told how he got out of jail.

Sierra noticed the cross left from the old barn and the way the sun was shining on it. She thought to herself, 'I am truly blessed.'

WATCHING OVER ME

They were all sitting around on hay bales still talking.
Sierra stood up. "I'll see y'all tomorrow. I have to get a shower." She reached her hand out to Dallas.
Travis said, "You mean next week?"
She smiled at him and winked.
DC reached over and put Travis in a head lock and gave him a noogie.
Dallas took her hand and they walked to her cabin.

~~~~~

The next morning, Dallas stood in the doorway and watched her sleep. He was so grateful to have her back in his life safe and sound. He cooked her breakfast and was ready to serve her. He placed the engagement ring on a serving tray when he heard her get up.
"Good morning," she rubbed her eyes.
"Good morning sleepy head," he walked over to embrace her.
"I was so tired." She was wearing her white silky gown. They slow danced in the kitchen for a while. "Did you cook breakfast casserole?"
"I did," he lifted her chin up, "but you have to go back to bed

to get it."

"Breakfast in bed? Only if you join me."

"Of course," he danced her to the bedroom. Then he fluffed the pillows and swept her off her feet and placed her on the bed.

"I like this kind of service."

"I'm a full-service man. I'll be right back." When he came back, he set the tray over her. She patted the bed next to her. He half laid down beside her and propped on his elbow. She lifted the tray cover and gasped when she saw her ring. She covered her lips with her hand. "Are you sure?" They looked at each other.

"I've never been more sure about anything in my life as I'm sure about living the rest of my life with you." He took the ring off the tray. "I'm asking you again, will you marry me?"

She turned toward him and took his face in her hands and kissed him.

"Is that a yes?"

"Yes, you know it is." She held out her finger.

He placed the ring on her finger.

"After last night, did you have any doubt?"

"Just making sure." Dallas kissed her hand.

~~~~~

Later that day Burt said, "I didn't expect to see y'all today."

They looked at each other and smiled.

"We have the rest of our lives to make up for lost time," she held up her hand with the ring on it.

"Good, I'm glad you got that worked out."

Dallas kissed her. "Her love is like a force field. Once you're inside of it, you never want to escape."

"You say the sweetest things," she squeezed his hand.

"The FBI will be here in about an hour. We need to give them all the evidence. Now let's finish this," Burt said.

"There's one more thing I have to do before this goes down."

"What's that?" Dallas asked.

"Get Sprocket back. Johnny said they have him in the Chalet."

James said, "They're going to be ready with guns blazing. Are you sure you want to start a war on the mountain."

"They won't be ready for what I have planned," Sierra grinned.

~~~~~

The FBI arrived and they were given all the evidence.

"The drugs are not at the concrete company. It would be better if we actually had the drugs."

Sierra thought a minute. "Let's just say I have concrete evidence." She took the men to the concrete poured at the river. "If you analyze this, you'll find what you need. It's a special blend."

They started breaking off pieces of concrete.

~~~~~

The next day, Sierra came out in insulated camo and her face was painted.

Dallas said, "You can't break and enter."

"I don't plan to." She walked up to Duke. "Duke is. Do you think they'll arrest a horse?" She laughed.

"No," he laughed.

"Duke doesn't need a saddle; I'll ride him bareback." She put a trick saddle on Raindancer and put a book bag over the horn. "Sprocket will be in this."

They put every trick saddle they had on a horse.

Johnny said, "You be careful. Time to warrior up."

"That's right. I will, you just watch for Duke and Raindancer to come down Lucifer Ridge side. I'll be coming down Paradise side to create a distraction for Duke and Raindancer."

Johnny asked, "How are you getting to the other side of the river?"

"The zip line. Burt, are you sure where to put all the horses on that side?" She tightened a belly strap.

"Most will be on Paradise Point. One when you get off the zip line."

Burt said, "I hope you can run fast to get to that zip line."

"Dallas says I run like a deer," and they looked at each other. "Lord, make me run like a deer today."

"You know you don't have to do this?" Burt looked at her.

"I tried to tell her," Dallas said.

"Yes, I do." She petted Duke on the neck.

Burt smiled at her. "Artemis."

She smiled back at him. "God's gonna' watch over me."

James said, "We'll be ready for what comes our way."

Dallas said, "I love you. Do everything in love." They kissed.

"And I'll walk through fire for you. GV GE YU (I love you)."

He helped her mount Duke. She nudged Duke in the ribs and took off up the mountain, leading Raindancer.

~~~~~

Once at the chalet, Sierra hid Raindancer. She walked Duke to the front door and knocked. When they opened the door, they stood in bewilderment. "What the hell?"

"Sprocket, come here boy," followed by a loud whistle. Sprocket ran out the door and jumped in her arms. "Let's go boy." She put him in the backpack and slung it onto her back.

Duke reared up and pawed at the man. Duke kept them preoccupied as Sierra ran to Raindancer. She slapped him on the hind quarter. "Go home, boy." She whistled for Duke. She slapped him on the hind quarter as he ran by her.

~~~~~

Sierra took off running across the mountain toward the river.

The elk that came to her in the river began to run alongside her through the woodland.

Several men took off after her too, and fired their pistols toward her.

She reached the zip line and grabbed the pulley. In her haste she failed to see the zip line had been loosened. When she got over the river, it pulled loose from the trees and in the raging river she fell. The water was ice cold, and it took her breath away. She gasped for air, as she fought against the current, but it was too strong.

The elk plunged himself into the river.

The suction pulled her downstream toward the waterfall and certain death. She held tight to the cable as the current sucked her downstream. She cried out, "Jesus!"

The elk's antlers caught in the zip line as he exited the river. He twisted around the cable trying to shake it free.

Sierra held with all her might as she went over the edge of the falls and the water rushed over her. The force of the water hurled her outward, but she held tight through a blinding jerk and back through the waterfall, landing underneath the overhanging rock.

She knelt on the ground, shocked she was still alive and shivering. She gasped for air. "Thank you, Lord." She shed the wet coveralls and made her way under the river to the other side. She climbed over rocks and through the woods.

She whistled for the horse at the end of the zip line, but he couldn't hear her over the roar of the river.

The men saw her. "This girl just won't die. We need the

chopper."

She continued to climb through the woods and up the steep embankment. She pulled herself up on the tree roots and over hanging branches. She whistled again for the horse. This time he heard her call. He ran to her, and she mounted him. They reached Paradise Point, and she changed horses and whistled for the others to follow. They ran down the mountainous terrain together toward the ranch.

The men hovered over her in the chopper like a fire breathing dragon as the flames rained down around them. The underbrush began to burn.

The smoke became thick, but in the cover of the smoke she would change horses and do trick riding to avoid the bullets. Each time they would have to find her again.

~~~~~

Everyone at the ranch could tell from the chopper she was in trouble. They were ready and waiting with their own fire power. Soon as the chopper was in firing distance, they returned fire.

Fire was beginning to rage on the mountain. The men continued to fire back until the chopper retreated to the other side of the mountain.

Sierra and the herd submerged from the smoke and blaze out into the pasture.

~~~~~

Johnny met Raindancer and Duke on the other side of the ranch. Sprocket made it home at last.

~~~~~

The FBI arrived at the ranch. Sierra told them, "Tonight is a huge party at the casino. You better have your people in place, 'cause tonight is the night. They. Go. Down!" She pointed her finger at the man in charge.

~~~~~

Sierra put on some brown leather pants and a jacket with fringe, and her outback coat on top of that. She and Duke crossed over the mountain and down the other side in the fresh snow on the ski slope.

~~~~~

The casino was full. The Chinese and CEOs were all there. Anne was on stage. "The ski slopes are now officially open!"

Sierra gave her outback coat to the valet and turned Duke right

through the door.
The crowd moved out of her way.

~~~~~

She burst through the ballroom doors on Duke. She marched him toward the stage.

"Who do you think you are coming in here on that wretched animal! Guards!" Anne was screaming.

People were gasping and screaming but continued to move out of her way.

Sierra and Duke made their way up the steps onto the stage.

"Who are you!" one of them said.

Sierra dismounted and walked toward Anne. Anne started backing away from her. "Guards!"

The other men were wandering around on the stage and looked for an escape route.

Sierra punched Anne in the mouth, and she went flying backward. "That's for stealing my dog!"

"Who are you?" Carlos Cilia asked.

She climbed back on to Duke.

"I'm nobody! The only name you need to know is…JESUS! That's the only name that matters. You can think about that while you all sit in prison a few years."

They laughed at her.

The FBI drew out their guns and pointed them at the criminals.

Duke reared up ready to slug somebody.

The crowd began to applaud.

Dallas and Sierra's eye met.

Dallas gave her a thumbs up, "She did it. It's finally done."

Burt clapped as he yelled, "You got 'em, girl!"

LEATHER AND LACE

Things were slow at the ranch during winter, so Sierra started working at the clinic almost every day.

"Emily, I'm going to head home. I need you to give this to Dallas in about thirty minutes. He's busy and he has a couple more clients to see." She handed her an envelope.

"Okay, sure."

"Don't forget, thirty minutes."

"What is it? If you don't mind me asking."

She grinned shyly and pulled her ear lobe. "Just a picture of me."

"Oooh, I get it," she shook her head slowly and grinned.

"When he comes out next time…" She hesitated.

"Yeah."

"…ask him if he rabbit hunts."

"Okay." Emily grinned.

Sierra left the clinic without saying anything to Dallas.

Dallas came out and asked, "Where's Sierra?"

"She left, but she said to ask you if you rabbit hunt."

He looked puzzled and put his thumb and forefinger to his chin. He didn't answer and walked away.

Emily sat there smiling and watched the clock carefully.

Dallas came out later with a client.

"Sierra said to give you this," she handed him the envelope.

He pulled the picture out. His eyes got big, and he grinned from ear to ear. "Follow the clues." She had kissed it with red lipstick. He looked at his watch. "This is going to be a long thirty minutes."

In the picture, she was sitting in his truck with a long stem red rose over her shoulder. Dallas finished work as fast as he could. He ran out the door and got in his truck. There was a red rose and a rabbit pelt waiting for him in the seat. There was another envelope with red lipstick on it. He pulled out another picture. She was on his horse, Comet.

~~~~~

Dallas hurried home and went straight to Comet. In his stall was another envelope with lipstick and a rabbit pelt. He pulled out the picture and drove to the house.

~~~~~

He went straight to his motorcycle. He gathered pictures throughout his house and rabbit pelts. The last picture was her in his bed. He opened the door to his bedroom, and he stood there biting his bottom lip and grinned from ear to ear. She had feathers in her hair.

"Hello, honey bunny," she bit her own lip.

He slowly walked toward her as he ran his fingers through his hair. "Nice guitar," he reached for it and set it against the wall.

"You needed a new one, so you can sing to me in our little love nest." Fur was all around her. "I have one more picture for you." She handed it to him.

~~~~~

The next day, Dallas and Sierra were decorating the Christmas tree and the FBI knocked on the door. Sierra opened it. "Hello, come in." She began to move some boxes out of the way.

"Congratulations, we got 'em. It goes from China, through Mexico, Texas, and beyond."

Sierra and Dallas smiled at each other as they hugged.

"We could have never done it without all your evidence. They will be in prison for a long time."

"Good, they deserve it." Sierra smiled.

"There's still a huge need for a person with your skills."

Sierra looked at Dallas. "What do you mean?"

"If you want to come work with us, you've got a job waiting for you."

"Thanks, but no thanks. I've found where I belong unless I'm forced again," she winked at him.

He nodded, "I understand."

She leaned toward his ear and whispered something.

That night on the news it showed a Texas congressman and his staff being arrested for drug trafficking.

~~~~~

Sierra rode to Paradise Point and took a knee in front of the burned cross from the barn.

"Dear Heavenly Father, thank you for your grace and mercy and my gift. You've blessed me in so many ways, when I didn't deserve it. You watched over me, when I needed you most. Forgive those that have sinned against me. Burden their hearts to accept you as their personal Savior. Thank you for my family and all those who have stood by me. Thank you for letting me be raised in a Christian home and to know Jesus as my Lord and Savior. Thank you, Lord, for dying on the cross for the sins of this world, and for showing me life has a chance with you in our hearts. Help me to be a better person, to walk in your light and show the world that your love is real. Help me to do everything in love. In your holy and precious name, I pray. Amen."

~~~~~

After Christmas, everyone was super busy to get ready for the January 10th wedding of Dallas Clayton Davenport and Abigail Diana Sierra Turner-Wilson.

Icicle lights were hung in the trees and Christmas trees were placed against a backdrop of the purple mountains. The evergreen trees were decorated in red and white.

The guys all wore black tuxes and cowboy hats. Travis was the best man, Taylor and Tyler stood next to him.

The girls wore red dresses and covered their shoulders with white fur shawls. They had on long white gloves and carried red and white amaryllises.

Travis and Kate stared at each other the whole time.

One of the white horses' mane was braided with white ribbon, white and silver beads. The horse blanket was red, and ribbons hung from the edges.

Sierra approached sitting to the side.

James and Johnny helped her off the horse.

She took a deep breath as she took Burt by the arm.

He winked at her.

Dallas could not believe his eyes as she walked forward to greet her groom. Their hearts pounded like thunder once again.

Sierra's hair was straight with a head piece on the side made of ribbon and feathers with silver and white beads. Her dress was a tightly fitted bodice of white faux leather. At the top was white fur and ribbons of white and silver beads dangled from the fur. The bodice came to a V in front, with ribbons and beads hanging around its edge. The back was laced with white ribbon and her skin showed through the laces. At the bottom of the laces was more white fur, feathers, beads and ribbon that hung way down the train. The bottom and long train of faux leather was covered with lace overlay and around the edges were gathered. Fur and beads were placed all around the gathers. Her moccasin fur boots had fringe of beads at the top and on the toe were beads.

Sierra and Dallas were each wrapped in blue blankets.

They had written their own vows to each other and when it came time to kiss, the snow began to fall. The blue blankets were taken away and they were wrapped together in one white blanket to show unity.

~~~~~

At the reception they danced, but Sierra had another skirt to change into. It was short and split up the side and overlapped. Beaded fringe went all around the edges. On one side was the piece from the back of her dress with fur, feathers, ribbons, and beads.

~~~~~

That summer there was a rodeo at the ranch for the first time in sixteen years.

The announcer said, "Give a big welcome to Abigail Turner Davenport in a tribute to her parents, Gayle and Tom Turner."

She had on the top of her wedding dress and white leather pants.

There were huge screens in the background with the beach and waves in motion.

She walked out in the arena and knelt before a cross.

The announcer read 'Footprints in the Sand.'

She rode Roman style on her Andalusian horses and weaved them back and forth like her mom used to do. Their manes and tails were braided in ribbons and beads.

Then fire was lit up everywhere in the arena and on the screens.

Bam-Bam was released.

She grabbed the muleta and had a playful bullfight with Bam-Bam. She laid in the dirt with Bam-Bam hovering over her. The lights and fire went out.

The audience gasped and came to their feet.

Sierra put on the bottom of her wedding dress.

Three of the white horses entered the arena and came to her. Two of them went into a prayer position.

She positioned herself across the two horses.

The lead horse reared up. The other two followed and they encircled the arena in sync as they carried her. Her parents' pictures appeared on the big screen.

Then Sierra moved to the lead horse and stood on his back, with her white gown flowing in the breeze, as she encircled the arena. She held her arm high in the air for victory. She exited the arena.

The announcer said, "Sierra, can you please return to the center of the arena."

"What's going on?" as she looked at her family and dismounted the horse.

Dallas took her hand, and they all went to the center. They were joined by the Tribal Council.

Little did Sierra know that Burt, Johnny, and the FBI had written letters to the Tribal Council.

Sierra squeezed Dallas' hand with both of her hands as they approached the Tribal Councilmen.

"Sierra, you have gone to great lengths unselfishly to build up your community with your own money. You bravely rescued twelve girls from three other countries that were being held against their will. You have brought down ruthless drug cartels, and in doing so, saved countless individuals and communities throughout several countries. You have saved many lives. We proudly present you with this headdress for your bravery." He placed the full-length headdress on her head. "This is a great honor to our people, so wear it with pride. You earned it. May you always be a leader to your people and a great warrior."

You could hear people from the wolf clan howling over the applause.

EPILOGUE

Dallas and Sierra rode together bareback to the top of Lucifer Ridge and looked out over the land.

Dallas' face was buried in her hair, his arms around her, the reins in his hands.

Sierra said, "I heard the EBCI bought the casino and I know of a nice chalet for sale."

"Well, I heard some rich lady bought the ski slopes." He laid his chin on her shoulder.

"How does Lucifer Ridge Roller Coaster and Ski Slopes sound?" She turned to look at him.

"You're gonna have to help run it though."

"You know I will of course, we're in this together and you should know by now I support you even when you have some crazy ideas." He hugged her a little tighter. "I do have one question that's been on my mind."

"Oh, and what's that?"

"Do you remember that day the FBI offered you a job and you whispered something to him?"

"Yes."

"What did you say to him?"

"I told him to find my missing indigenous sisters, or I will."

Made in the USA
Columbia, SC
03 July 2023